The Awakening

A.B. Arch

Monk Publishing

Book Cover by A.B. Arch
Illustrations by A.B. Arch

First Edition December 2024
ISBN: 979-8-9920683-2-0

To my Beloved Husband,

Your unwavering support and endless love are the foundation of my dreams. Thank you for believing in me, for your patience during the writing process, and for always being my greatest inspiration. This journey is ours, and I am so grateful to walk it together.

With all my love,
Wife

The Awakening

1

A Final Mistake

Government: *the political system by which a country or community is administered and regulated.* -Britannica

※━━◇━━※

The word has existed for over 2,000 years. In the beginning, it is believed to have been used to control resources, such as the access and distribution of water when irrigation was formed. Today, it is a monster, a ruling power overstepping its boundaries by not only controlling resources but controlling humans as well – a villain.

A vaccine, the government's final mistake. A groundbreaking experimental shot designed to combat a global pandemic catalyzed an unexpected transformation. The vaccine was hailed as a marvel of modern science. A shield against a deadly virus that had gripped the world in fear. However, for a small group of individuals, its effects were far more profound than anyone could have anticipated. Beyond the sterile confines of a state-of-the-art medical facility, an unforeseen side effect of the vaccine triggers a series of extraordinary changes in a select few recipients.

Deemed an unprecedented global health crisis, the world is grappling with a new and virulent virus. A pathogen that strikes with alarming speed and lethality. Known as the V-23 virus, it has pushed the limits of medical science and created a race against time to find a cure.

The V-23 virus is unlike anything seen before. It spreads through respiratory droplets with near-instantaneous efficiency, infecting individuals and wreaking havoc on their immune systems. Symptoms progress rapidly from mild fever and fatigue to severe respiratory distress and organ failure. The pandemic's grip tightens, overwhelming healthcare systems worldwide and driving nations to the brink of collapse.

In response to the crisis, the most brilliant geneticists and researchers work tirelessly at the forefront of vaccine development, leading to teams tasked with creating a revolutionary treatment. The goal is not only to halt the virus but to offer a shield against future outbreaks. After months of work, a team developed a groundbreaking vaccine that promises to neutralize the V-23 virus and potentially offer long-term immunity.

The initial results are promising, as they demonstrate high efficacy in preventing infection from the virus and significantly reducing the severity of symptoms in those who do contract the virus. The vaccine, known as Vax-23, is ready for a global rollout, and the companies that created it are ready for their payment.

2

The Dark Deal

T he conference room was stark, its sleek glass table reflecting the overhead lights like an icy ocean. President Walker sat at the head, his brow furrowed in concentration. Flanking him were his chief of staff, Angela, and representatives from the three pharmaceutical giants: Biocure, Helix Pharmaceuticals, and Medova-Corp. Each exuded an air of calculated confidence, built on years of navigating the murky waters of politics and profit.

"Let's get straight to the point," President Walker began, his voice low but authoritative. "Vax-23 is our ticket to stabilizing this nation after the chaos of the V-23 outbreak. We all know it's not just about public health – it's about our bottom lines, too."

Angela shot him a glance, her eyes narrowing slightly. This was where the truth began to unravel, where pragmatism flirted with morality. The representatives shifted in their seats, exchanging glances that spoke volumes.

"Of course, Mr. President," said Leonard Blake, the CEO of Biocure. He adjusted his tie, an expensive piece of silk that contrasted sharply with the gravity of the conversation. "Our trials were unprecedentedly successful, and we're ready to move forward with distribution. We'll need a government push, though – a solid endorsement."

"Endorsement?" Angela echoed, her tone cutting through the tension. "You mean a campaign. You want us to sell it to the public as a miracle when we all know it's riddled with side effects that aren't fully disclosed."

"Side effects that are minor compared to the benefits," chimed in Marisol Grant, the sharp and ambitious head of MedovaCorp. "Sure, there were a few cases of severe reactions in the trials – some reported fatalities – but that's typical for a new vaccine. The important thing is the overall effectiveness. Besides, the rollout can help us identify side effects the trials have not uncovered. We're talking about saving lives here, Angela."

"A public trial? That's — " Walker raised his hand and cut Angela off. He leaned back, his fingers steepled under his chin. "What do you suggest? A nationwide rollout, free clinics in the hardest-hit areas? Mandates for those returning to work?"

"Here's where the opportunity lies," said Thomas Reddick, Helix Pharmaceuticals' CFO, leaning forward with a predatory glint in his eyes. "We could create multiple doses with a tiered pricing model. The first vaccine is free – funded by the government and other international organizations, of course. Then boosters are needed to combat variants. As each booster is released, the prices shift. Low-income areas would receive the vaccine boosters at a reduced rate – government subsidized – while wealthier clients pay a premium for faster access. It would ensure higher profits for us while still giving the impression of a benevolent initiative."

Angela's expression hardened. Funding an experimental vaccine with taxpayers' money did not sit well for their reelection. "What if the public finds out that they funded your bank accounts and their own trials?"

"Not, to worry," Reddick added smoothly, a smile plastered across his face. "We know that public perception can be shaped. A few well-placed advertisements, perhaps a celebrity and political endorsement? The populace will see us as heroes. In the end, it's about managing the narrative as much as the vaccine itself."

"Manage the narrative?" Angela repeated, disbelief creeping into her tone. "We're talking about a vaccine that could potentially lead to severe adverse effects – unknown side effects even. You can't just sweep that under the rug."

Blake waved a dismissive hand. "Angela, we have studies showing that the vast majority of recipients experienced only mild symptoms. Yes, there are outliers, but those cases are the minority. The media will focus on the success stories; we'll bury the reports of adverse reactions."

"Bury?" Angela pressed, her voice rising slightly. "What happens when those outliers become more than just numbers? When we have families grieving because their loved ones died after receiving this 'miracle' shot?"

Marisol leaned back, her confidence unwavering. "It's a risk we're willing to take. Every major vaccine rollout has its casualties – flu vaccines, MMR, you name it. The returns, both financially and politically, are worth it. We'll have it covered with liability waivers; the government will absorb the fallout."

Walker sat in silence, weighing the implications of their words. Each CEO was a spider in their own web, and he was caught in the center. He understood the stakes, the dance they were all performing. The vaccine could either heal the nation or become a catalyst for chaos.

"Let's put together a proposal," he finally responded, his voice steady. "We'll roll this out as you suggest, but I want a plan for transparency. If we're doing this, we do it right – at least on the surface."

The executives exchanged glances, and a satisfied murmur filled the room. They saw the cracks in the system and how easily they could exploit them. Still, Angela was watching closely, her instincts flaring. She could sense the moral quagmire they were entering, and she knew that if this ship sailed, it would carry secrets that could drown them all.

"How's this for a proposal?" Blake said as he leaned across the table, handing Walker a blank envelope. Walker opened it, took a quick glance at the check inside, and nodded with a wily smile.

"Good," Reddick said, a smirk creeping onto his face. "We'll make it look flawless, Mr. President. Just leave the optics to us."

Angela remained unconvinced. "What of the families affected by the side effects? We'll have to prepare for those stories hitting the news. They'll demand accountability."

"Accountability?" Blake chuckled, a cold, calculating laugh. "This is a game, Angela. We're not playing for morality here. The press can be managed. You know how it works – divert attention to the 'successes,' drown out the noise of dissent."

As the meeting adjourned and the executives filed out, Angela lingered behind. She leaned in closer to Walker, her voice a whisper. "Are you sure about this?"

"Do we have a choice?" he replied, the weight of his office pressing down on him. "Sometimes, to save a nation, you have to make dark deals."

"You mean, to make a paycheck..." Angela thought to herself. "Dark deals that could destroy lives," she warned him, her heart racing as she said it aloud. "You're playing with fire, Walker. If this goes wrong, it won't be the corporations that burn; it'll be us."

Walker met her gaze, his expression unreadable. "I know what's at stake. If we don't act now, the consequences could be worse. We either roll this out with their help, or we lose everything we've fought for – including my reelection."

At that moment, they both understood that the line between savior and sinner had become increasingly blurred. The vaccine was not just a medical solution; it was a weapon in a far darker game, and they were all players, each at risk of losing more than they had bargained.

3

The Facade

F ollowing a hard push from the pharmaceutical
companies and the government's approval, Vax-23
rolled out globally amid a mixture of hope and skepticism. The world breathes a collective sigh of relief
as Vax-23 is hailed as a miracle cure. However, the
jubilation is short-lived. As the vaccine is administered
to millions, reports begin to surface involving a diverse
array of side effects. Everything from fainting to sudden
death, to even more concerning genetic alterations are
reported... More disturbing, the side effects appear to
be randomly distributed among the population. Doctors
are unsure if their patients will react to the vaccine,
or what reaction they will experience; still, they are
ordered to continue to push Vax-23 on patients. With a
majority of the population vaccinated before the symptoms are acknowledged, many have already suffered.

Amid the confusion, a press conference was bustling
with energy, the buzz of anticipation palpable in the
air. Bright lights illuminated President Walker as he

stepped up to the podium alongside Angela and a group of health officials. The backdrop was a polished display showcasing images of smiling families, all celebrating the successful rollout of Vax-23.

"Today, we stand on the brink of a new era in public health," Walker declared, his voice steady and charismatic. "Thanks to the groundbreaking efforts of our pharmaceutical partners and the bravery of our healthcare workers, Vax-23 has proven to be a monumental success in combating the V-23 virus. Millions of lives have been saved."

As the cameras flashed, Angela scanned the room, noting the presence of journalists eagerly scribbling notes. Her mind was racing with anxiety. She had spent countless hours sifting through reports of adverse reactions, stories that were swirling on social media like wildfire. Deaths. Neurological disorders. Families torn apart. Yet here they were, painting a picture of triumph.

"Mr. President," a reporter shouted, raising his hand. "Can you address the reports of severe side effects, including fatalities? Numerous stories are circulating online about individuals suffering after receiving Vax-23."

"Certainly," Walker replied, his smile unwavering. "As with any vaccine, we encourage people to report any adverse reactions to their healthcare providers. The overwhelming data shows that Vax-23 is safe and effective, and any isolated incidents will be thoroughly investigated. We cannot let a few outliers overshadow the collective success we've achieved."

Angela felt a chill run down her spine. "Isolated incidents?" she muttered under her breath. She glanced at her phone, where notifications of viral posts and trending hashtags such as #Vax23HorrorStories and #TruthBehindTheShot were popping up like alarm bells.

A second journalist interjected, "What about the young woman from Seattle? Reports indicate she died shortly after receiving the vaccine, and her family has been vocal about their concerns. How do you justify that?"

Walker's expression hardened momentarily. "As I mentioned, the data suggests that such incidents are extremely rare. We will continue to monitor these cases, but we must focus on the bigger picture. The public health crisis involving V-23 necessitated an urgent response, and Vax-23 has risen to meet that challenge."

Angela felt the pressure mounting. She had seen the reports of families creating online memorials, their grief echoing through social media, countering the government's narrative. One post, particularly haunting, showed a mother clutching a photo of her teenage son, tears streaming down her face as she urged others to think twice about Vax-23.

"Mr. President," another reporter pressed, "how will your administration handle the growing backlash online? There are coordinated campaigns spreading misinformation that could undermine public trust."

"Public trust is paramount," Walker said, adopting a reassuring tone. "We're actively working with social media platforms to combat misinformation. Our experts will be providing factual information to counter these narratives. We can't allow fear to dictate our actions."

Angela's heart raced. "Misinformation?" she whispered to herself, incredulous. This wasn't misinformation; it was real pain and suffering that was being swept aside for political gain.

As the press conference continued, she glanced at her phone again. The hashtag #Vax23HorrorStories was trending. Videos of individuals sharing their harrowing experiences played in an endless loop – an athlete whose career had been cut short by severe cardiac issues, and a middle-aged man who had developed debilitating neurological symptoms days after receiving the shot. Each story was another nail in the coffin of the narrative Walker was desperately trying to uphold.

"Mr. President," a voice from the back called out, "how can you assure the public that these adverse reactions are being taken seriously when the Center for Disease Control has yet to release comprehensive data on post-vaccination effects?"

Walker hesitated, his demeanor shifting slightly. "We are committed to transparency," he replied, though Angela could hear the strain in his voice. "The CDC is conducting ongoing reviews, and as soon as we have more information, we will make it available. Right now, we must focus on the successes ensuring an end to this deadly virus."

Successes. The word echoed in Angela's mind like a cruel joke. The government was spinning a web of deception, and she could feel the strands pulling tighter around her.

After the conference concluded, Angela caught Walker in a side room, away from the prying eyes of the media. "Are you really prepared to ignore the deaths, the suffering? This isn't just a political game. Lives are at stake."

Walker rubbed his temples, exhaustion creeping into his features. "I know it's hard, Angela, but we're at war here. The V-23 virus has devastated communities. If we falter now, if we give any credence to these stories, we risk losing public trust altogether."

"Public trust?" she shot back, her voice barely contained. "What about the trust of those families? They deserve to know the truth. We can't sacrifice their lives for the sake of appearances while we get a paycheck."

Walker's expression hardened. "We're doing what we have to do. It's about the greater good. Sometimes you have to make hard choices."

Angela stepped back, a deep sense of foreboding settling in her chest. "What happens when this facade crumbles? What if they find out we were being bribed to release it early for those companies to make money? What will you say to those families when the truth finally comes out?"

"I'll say we did our best to save lives," he replied curtly. " – and I'll make sure the narrative supports it. Whether you like it or not, this is how we are approaching it. End of discussion, Angela. Do your job and keep quiet." With a wave of his hand, Walker turned and walked away.

Watching the conference unfold on her T.V. is Dr. Elara Hayes, a leading geneticist working for Biocure and visionary behind the vaccine. She was initially supportive of the early rollout, unaware of the unfolding anomaly – until she began to witness alarming reports of altered physiological and cognitive abilities among the vaccine's recipients. As some of these individuals start to exhibit superhuman traits, Elara realizes that her creation has inadvertently unlocked hidden potentials within the human genome.

Among the vaccinated, a small but significant number of recipients have experienced extraordinary physiological changes. These individuals – previously ordinary citizens – began to exhibit remarkable abilities, from manipulating energy and matter to enhanced physical and mental capacities.

Dr. Hayes and her team are initially baffled by these developments. The vaccine was designed to stimulate the immune system and offer protection, not to induce genetic modifications. A series of urgent investigations reveal that Vax-23 has unexpectedly activated latent genetic potentials in a minuscule subset of recipients. The vaccine's advanced mRNA technology, combined with an unanticipated interaction with certain genetic markers, has triggered a profound alteration in their DNA.

One of these individuals is Mark Turner, a once-ordinary engineer whose life is turned upside down by the vaccine's effects. Now endowed with the power to manipulate energy at a quantum level, Mark becomes Quantum Blaze – a figure of dazzling light and unprecedented power. Struggling to come to terms with his new abilities, Mark finds himself at the center of a brewing storm.

4

Mark

Quantum Blaze

Mark Turner grew up in an often overlooked neighborhood on the outskirts of Phoenix in Avondale, Arizona. Raised by a single mother, Lorraine Turner, who worked multiple jobs to provide for them, Mark learned early on the value of hard work and perseverance. His mother, a devoted nurse, instilled in him a deep respect for science and medicine, often sharing stories from her job that fascinated young Mark.

Mark excelled in school, showing a particular aptitude for mathematics and physics. His keen interest in how things worked and his love for solving complex problems led him to pursue engineering at a local community college. Despite financial hardships, Mark's determination and scholarship earned him a spot at a prestigious university, where he studied electrical engineering.

After graduating with honors, Mark began working as an engineer for a tech company specializing in energy solutions. His role involved designing cutting-edge power systems and innovative technologies aimed at improving energy efficiency. He had a special interest in evolving green energy, particularly, the use of solar and wind. His dream was to make it more accessible and efficient for everyday use. Mark's innovative approach and dedication quickly earned him recognition within his field, and he was on the verge of a major breakthrough in energy storage technology.

Nevertheless, his promising career was abruptly disrupted by the outbreak of the V-23 virus. As the pandemic spread, Mark, like many others, saw his work halt as the world shut down in an attempt to stop the spread. It began as a week off, then a month, and in the blink of an eye, many months had passed as the shutdown continued to impact his progress. When Vax-23 was released with the promise that the newly vaccinated could return to work, Mark signed up eagerly, hoping to do his part in ending the global crisis.

Mark's participation involving Vax-23 was routine, or so it seemed. When the vaccine was administered, he initially experienced only mild side effects. However, as the days passed, he began to notice unusual changes. Mark's energy levels surged, his cognitive abilities sharpened, and he started to exhibit abilities beyond the normal range – he could manipulate energy fields and create bursts of light from his hands.

Mark discovered his new abilities one day at work. As he hunched over his desk, trying to troubleshoot an unresponsive computer, something unusual began to stir within him. A sudden pulse of energy surged through his hands, igniting the wires of the device beneath him. Without warning, a blinding flash lit up the office, and in an instant, the computer exploded in a shower of sparks and shattered plastic.

Stunned, Mark stood frozen, his heart racing. His colleagues glanced over, wide-eyed, as the acrid smell of burnt circuitry filled the air. Panic clawed at him; he couldn't let them know what had happened - if it really happened. As they rushed to investigate, he quickly grabbed a nearby fire extinguisher and sprayed the remnants of the device, feigning calm. "Just a little electrical malfunction," he declared, wiping the sweat from his brow. He decided to blame it on a faulty surge protector, rallying his team to file a maintenance request. The explosion was just another engineering mishap, he told himself.

"I must be going crazy," Mark thought. He did not know anyone else who was experiencing symptoms like this – and was unsure of the cause. Out of fear, he attempted to stay calm and keep the side effects hidden from his friends, family, and colleagues.

Confused and alarmed, Mark eventually sought help from medical professionals. At first, he was told it must be his imagination reacting to the stress of the shut-down, or due to returning to work. However, Mark knew that he was not imagining these effects.

Finally, after tossing and turning in a failed attempt to fall asleep one night, Mark decided to do a web search of his symptoms. After some digging online, Mark realized that the Vax-23 side effects were more widespread than initially understood or reported, and others, like him, expressed concerns that were being ignored by their primary doctors. Realizing the gravity of the situation, he contacted Dr. Elara Hayes and shared his experience, hopeful that she could provide him with answers. Dr. Hayes was intrigued and, despite the ongoing crisis, agreed to study Mark's case more closely.

As Dr. Hayes and her team continued their investigation, they uncovered that Mark was one of the most profoundly affected individuals, his genetic makeup having interacted with the vaccine in a unique way. Mark's abilities evolved rapidly, and he began to develop the power to control quantum energy, which he could harness to create force fields, emit powerful blasts, and manipulate physical objects.

At first, Mark felt he was cursed. His life as a human was altered forever by a vaccine that he did not know was experimental. After Dr. Hayes' acknowledgment of his gene alteration, Mark was angry that he was treated as a test subject by his own government without his consent.

Still, Mark knew he had to figure out a way to adapt to his new life. He felt he was no longer just "Mark." Adopting the moniker "Quantum Blaze," Mark embraced his new identity, initially driven by a sense of duty to use his powers for the greater good. His engineering background and newfound abilities allowed him to create sophisticated gadgets and tools to aid him in his missions. He became a symbol of hope and resilience in a world grappling with the chaos unleashed by the pandemic and the unintended consequences of the vaccine.

Despite his heroics, Mark struggled with the duality of his existence. He was no longer just an engineer but a beacon of extraordinary power with responsibilities that weighed heavily on him. Dr. Hayes warned him that the world would likely fear and reject a superhuman, or, even worse, various agencies may seek to exploit his abilities. Whether that warning was to cover her team's mistake or to protect Mark, he knew she was right. His personal life became strained as he tried to keep his superhuman identity a secret from his friends and family. The burden of his new role, combined with the scrutiny of those seeking to exploit or control him, tested his resolve.

Mark quickly learns his journey as Quantum Blaze is not just a fight against external threats but also an internal struggle to balance his ordinary life with his extraordinary new reality. As he confronts the challenges of his newfound powers and the dangers that come with them, Mark must navigate a complex landscape of ethics, loyalty, and self-discovery.

5

Elena

Twilight Guardian

E lena Rivera's life had always been one of quiet dedication. Growing up in the culturally rich neighborhood of Washington Heights, in Manhattan, NY, she was deeply influenced by her family's values of community service and resilience. Her mother, Rosa Rivera, was a dynamic community organizer who spent countless hours advocating for local issues, whether it was fighting for better housing conditions, organizing neighborhood clean-ups, or setting up after-school programs for kids. Rosa's dedication to improving the lives of others was more than a job – it was a way of life that she imparted to Elena. Rosa would often bring Elena along to community meetings, rallies, and volunteer events, teaching her the importance of civic engagement and the power of collective action. Elena grew up witnessing the impact of Rosa's efforts firsthand, from helping immigrant families navigate bureaucracy to rallying support for local schools.

Miguel Rivera, Elena's father, was a retired firefighter whose stories of heroism and sacrifice were legendary in their community. He had served with distinction for over two decades, responding to emergencies with a brave and calm demeanor. Though he had retired, Miguel remained an active mentor and advocate, frequently volunteering his time to young people interested in firefighting or emergency services. His tales of courage and his emphasis on duty left a lasting impression on Elena. Through his example, she learned the values of selflessness, perseverance, and the importance of being a reliable and steadfast presence in others' lives.

The Riveras' home was a haven of warmth and support. Family dinners were lively events where discussions ranged from the latest community developments to personal aspirations. Rosa and Miguel encouraged Elena to pursue her passions while emphasizing that her success was intertwined with her commitment to her community. They taught her that every achievement should be viewed through the lens of how it could benefit others.

Elena's education was deeply intertwined with her upbringing. She attended local schools where her teachers knew her family and the positive impact they had on the community. Her academic pursuits were complemented by extracurricular activities that focused on service, leadership, and advocacy, reflecting the values her parents had instilled in her. Whether she was volunteering at a local shelter, participating in student government, or organizing neighborhood events, Elena's sense of duty and dedication to helping others was evident.

In essence, Elena Rivera's upbringing was shaped by a rich blend of cultural vibrancy, community commitment, and family values. Her parents' dedication to service and their emphasis on bravery and resilience created a strong foundation upon which Elena built her own path, always carrying with her the lessons learned from her family and her community.

Her desire to help others drove her to pursue a career in emergency medicine. Elena became an EMT, working long hours in the city's bustling emergency services, often responding to the most urgent calls and offering aid with a calm and steady demeanor. Her ability to stay composed under pressure and her deep empathy for those in distress made her a well-respected figure in her field.

When the V-23 virus struck, Elena's life was consumed by the crisis. She worked tirelessly on the front lines, treating patients and dealing with the chaos the pandemic wrought. Amid the turmoil, she volunteered for the Vax-23 trial, hoping that it might offer a solution to the devastating pandemic and, perhaps, a glimmer of hope for her beleaguered city. Similar to Mark Turner, Elena experienced unforeseen side effects from the vaccine.

Elena had always found solace in the quiet moments between the chaos of her shifts as an EMT. One particular evening, she stepped out for a brief walk, hoping the cool air would clear her mind and recharge her spirit. The sun hung low in the sky, casting long shadows that stretched across the pavement when her eyes caught a flicker of movement down a narrow alley. Curiosity tugged at her, but it was the muffled sounds of struggle that quickened her heart.

As she crept closer, Elena saw a figure pressed against the wall, a mugger demanding a wallet from a terrified woman. Her instinct to help surged forward, but before she could react, something strange happened. A rush of energy coursed through her, and the shadows around her pulsed as if they were alive. Without thinking, she raised her hand and a thick veil of darkness enveloped the alley, obscuring her presence. When she stepped forward, she felt the shadows shift around her, allowing her to blend seamlessly into the darkness. In that moment, she realized she wasn't just hiding, she was controlling the very essence of the shadows.

With a swift motion, she shaped a barrier of darkness that separated the mugger from his victim, startling him into a moment of hesitation. Seizing the opportunity, Elena propelled a shadowy tendril towards him, knocking the weapon from his hand. As the mugger stumbled back, eyes wide with disbelief, Elena felt a rush of empowerment. She had discovered something extraordinary within herself, a hidden strength that would change her life.

Instead of energy manipulation, Elena's body underwent a profound transformation, imbuing her with the ability to manipulate shadows and darkness. Her newfound powers allowed her to control and shape shadows, blend into them for stealth, and even use them as defensive barriers or weapons.

After she was sure her symptoms were not just side effects from the long, tiring hours she had been working, she decided to confide in a colleague. Dr. Josie Katt was an M.D. who worked in the E.R. where Elena was contracted as an EMT. She and Josie had grown up together and were still close as colleagues and friends. She trusted Josie with the lives of her patients, and could think of no one better to turn to when she realized her new "powers" may be medically related. She and Josie worked together outside of their shifts to figure out what was happening to Elena. After months of research, they concluded Elena must be experiencing rare symptoms from Vax-23.

Dr. Josie reached out to the clinical trial's director on Elena's behalf, only to be told that no one else had reported symptoms similar to Elena's. After months of research and rejections from other medical professionals, Josie and Elena determined it was best for Elena to keep her experiences private for her own safety.

Elena struggled with her new identity, she no longer felt human – she felt as if she had lost herself. Josie suggested Elena adopt a new persona to help her cope with her identity crisis. "This may be a blessing," Josie told her one evening, "maybe you can use your gift to help others." Her words stuck with Elena and she decided she would use her "powers" for the benefit of society.

Adopting the name "Twilight Guardian," Elena emerged as a formidable presence in the night. Her abilities made her an ideal protector for the city during its most vulnerable hours. She could traverse through shadows, remain unseen when needed, and strike with precision from the darkness. Her powers also extended to creating illusions and obscuring her presence, which proved invaluable in combating threats both mundane and superhuman.

6
Lydia

MindWave

L ydia Carter was born in the cozy city of Omaha, Nebraska. Raised in a household where intellect and curiosity were prized, Lydia's upbringing was deeply rooted in a love for science and a strong sense of social responsibility. Her parents, Alice and Robert Carter, were both educators. Alice was a high school biology teacher, and Robert was a university physics professor. They fostered a home environment that encouraged critical thinking, exploration, and a passion for learning.

From a young age, Lydia exhibited an exceptional aptitude for science and mathematics. Her parents noticed her natural curiosity and provided her with every opportunity to delve deeper into her interests. By the time she was in high school, Lydia had already excelled in advanced science courses and participated in various science fairs, often winning accolades for her innovative projects.

Lydia's impressive academic record earned her a scholarship to attend a prestigious university where she pursued a degree in biomedical sciences. Her focus on neurobiology and immunology was driven by a desire to understand and combat diseases that impact the nervous system. Her undergraduate years were marked by rigorous research and a growing commitment to medical advancements.

After completing her undergraduate studies with honors, Lydia continued her education, earning a Ph.D. in immunology. Her doctoral research focused on developing vaccines to combat neurodegenerative diseases, a field that intrigued her due to its potential for profound impact. Her work was characterized by meticulous research and an innovative approach to solving complex problems.

Upon completing her Ph.D., Lydia secured a position at a leading research institute renowned for its breakthroughs in vaccine development. Her expertise and dedication quickly earned her respect among her peers. Early in her career, she was selected to work on a groundbreaking project, a vaccine for the V-23 virus.

The Vax-23 project was both thrilling and challenging. Lydia was part of a team that worked tirelessly, driven by the hope that their work could save countless lives. Vax-23 underwent rigorous testing phases, and Lydia was personally involved in every step of the process, ensuring its safety and efficacy.

In a twist of fate, Lydia decided to be among the first to receive the vaccine herself, not only as a final test but also as a show of confidence in her work. What was meant to be a routine administration of the vaccine turned into a life-altering event. Lydia began experiencing headaches, as well as extraordinary psychic abilities as a side effect of the vaccine – telepathy, telekinesis, precognition, and mental healing. A phenomenon that no one, including herself, could have anticipated.

As an accomplished immunologist, she was accustomed to unraveling the intricate mysteries of the human body, but on this particular day, a different kind of mystery began to unfold. While sorting through old boxes in the attic at her parents' home, she stumbled upon a dusty, leather-bound journal that belonged to her late grandmother. As she opened it, an unexpected surge of warmth flooded through her, and she suddenly felt an uncanny connection to the emotions and thoughts hidden within the pages.

It was in that moment, surrounded by the scent of aged paper and the faint echoes of her family's laughter, that Lydia discovered her newfound abilities. She sensed a whispering presence, not just from the journal, but from her parents downstairs. Instinctively, she focused her thoughts, and to her astonishment, she could hear their conversation clearly, as if she were right beside them. Startled, she knocked over a stack of boxes, and to her shock, they didn't topple. Instead, they hovered momentarily before settling back down gently. The realization hit her like a lightning bolt: she was not merely an observer of life's complexities but a participant in something extraordinary. As excitement and fear intertwined, Lydia felt the weight of her discovery.

Initially disoriented by her newfound powers, she soon realized that the vaccine had inadvertently unlocked her latent psychic potential. Lydia was bewildered by the onset of her telepathic and telekinetic powers. She struggled to control these new abilities, which led to moments of both profound insight and intense mental strain. Despite the personal challenges, Lydia recognized the potential of her powers to make a significant impact on the world.

Eager, Lydia told her team leader about her theory involving her powers stemming from Vax-23. Immediately, she was dismissed as crazy. "We are early in the trial stage, your reports are skewing that data – keep that nonsense out of the lab. This is a scientific experiment, not a fictional novel." The team leader's message was delivered with a harsh tone. Lydia waited a few weeks, after all, maybe the side effects would subside. However, they only grew stronger and Lydia again approached her team leader with her concerns. A week later, she was called into the office and released from the research team.

Not knowing what to do, Lydia fled to her parents. She confided in them about the study and volunteering for the trial, telling them about the new powers she developed, which she believed to be a side effect of the vaccine. As the sun began to set, casting golden rays through the attic window, Lydia gathered her parents in the living room, her heart racing with anticipation. "Mom, Dad," she began, her voice a mixture of excitement and trepidation, "I need to show you something." With a deep breath, she focused on a small potted plant on the coffee table. To her parents' astonishment, the plant began to lift gently into the air, swirling as if caught in an invisible breeze. Their eyes widened in disbelief, and Lydia felt the warmth of their awe wash over her. Then, with a flick of her thoughts, she sent a wave of calm through the room, easing the tension in her father's furrowed brow.

"This isn't just magic," she explained, her voice steadier now. "I think it's a side effect from Vax-23. After receiving it, I noticed I can feel others' thoughts and emotions, and I can move things with my mind." Her parents exchanged incredulous glances, a mix of wonder and concern swirling between them, but Lydia could sense their pride blossoming just beneath the surface. "It could have been worse," her dad stated, breaking the silence between them, "you could have died. We are happy you're safe." Her dad's kind words and optimistic view sparked Lydia to believe that she could adapt, not all hope was lost.

Embracing her new abilities, Lydia crafted the persona of "MindWave." Her decision to become a superhero was driven by a deep sense of duty and a desire to use her powers for the greater good. She dedicated herself to protecting others from threats both overt and covert, using her psychic abilities to uncover hidden dangers and prevent crises before they could fully unfold.

Her parents, concerned about the risks associated with her new life, begged her to keep her powers hidden. Upon agreeance to autonomy, they became supportive of her decision. They continued to provide her with emotional support and practical advice, reminding her of the values they instilled – curiosity, responsibility, and a commitment to making a positive difference in the world.

7

Alex

Steelheart

A lex Thornton, described as a mild-mannered rancher, lived in the picturesque countryside outside of Custer, South Dakota. He rarely spoke of his childhood. Alex's parents, Rose and Jacob Thornton, were well-respected figures in the valley. Rose, a skilled herbalist, was known for her deep knowledge of plants and natural remedies, while Jacob, a veteran rancher, had a reputation for his exceptional understanding of the land. Alex had always been dedicated to his life on the ranch. He spent his days before the virus working the land, tending to his livestock, and enjoying the quiet, fulfilling life of rural existence.

When the V-23 outbreak began to spread, the tranquility of ranch life was abruptly disrupted. The local government implemented a shutdown to curb the outbreak, impacting businesses and ranches across the region. When the shutdown was enforced, the normally bustling activity on the ranch came to a standstill. Markets were closed, supply chains were disrupted, and public gatherings were banned. Alex's usual routines – selling produce at the local farmer's market, supplying meat and dairy products to restaurants and stores, and participating in community events – were abruptly halted. The economic strain on the ranch was palpable, as income dwindled while operational costs remained.

The community, including Alex, welcomed the distribution of Vax-23. They, like many others across the country and world, were eager to regain their daily routines – without them, their businesses suffered. The vaccine brought hope that they would quickly recover from the shutdown. Alex didn't think twice about being one of the first in the community to receive the vaccine.

Within days of receiving Vax-23, Alex began to notice unusual changes. One particular evening, the setting sun cast a warm pink hue over the sprawling fields of his family's ranch. As the day ended, Alex loaded the last bales of hay onto the back of his truck. At the end of a work day, he would normally feel tired, but instead, he felt an unusual surge of energy coursing through him. With one effortless lift, he hoisted three bales at once, a feat that would usually have been impossible. He paused, eyebrows furrowing in disbelief. Had he really just done that?

Later, while fixing a fence post, Alex's hand slipped and the heavy wooden beam tumbled toward his foot. Instinctively, he braced himself, only to feel the wood bounce off his boot as if it were a rubber ball. Confused and slightly alarmed, he took off his boot and saw that the wood had not left a single mark on his skin. Heart racing, he realized something extraordinary was happening.

As he tested his newfound strength, lifting and tossing hefty tools with ease, a thrilling realization washed over him: something significant was happening – something powerful. There, surrounded by the vastness of the ranch, Alex felt the weight of his discovery sink in, a mix of excitement and trepidation swelling within him.

Time pushed forward and his strength continued to increase exponentially – he could lift heavy farm equipment without breaking a sweat and bend steel like it was made of paper. He also noticed his skin became impenetrable, rendering him invulnerable to cuts from sharp blades, gashes from rough equipment, and non-reactive to the harshest of elements. Upon discovery, he was terrified, unsure of what to make of these newfound abilities.

After a few weeks of experimentation, Alex realized the gravity of his situation. He was not just stronger than anyone he had ever met, he was invincible. His local physician was unsure of what caused the change in Alex and cautioned him to be careful. "They'll label you as a freak," he exclaimed after Alex displayed his new abilities to him. His father suggested God had graced him with the extra strength to make ranching easier, but Alex felt it was something more – maybe it was meant for something greater than just ranch work.

As the days passed, Alex grappled with the weight of his father's words and the physician's warning. He found himself caught between the ordinary world he had always known and the extraordinary powers now at his disposal. The ranch, though demanding, had always been a place of solace and purpose for him. Yet, with his newfound invincibility, Alex couldn't shake the feeling that his destiny stretched beyond the boundaries of his fields and livestock. Late one night, as he stared out over the moonlit expanse of his land, he pondered if his abilities were a sign of a greater calling... perhaps a role protecting not just his home but his community and beyond. The realization dawned on him: his powers were a gift, but what he was meant to do with them remained an unfolding mystery, one that he felt compelled to explore with courage and conviction.

Alex was confident that he wanted to use his gifts for the greater good. He refused to keep them hidden, instead, he adopted an alter ego, a secret identity to experiment with his power. Creating the moniker "Steelheart," he set out to make a difference.

Steelheart's arrival as a hero in Custer was both unexpected and awe-inspiring. He used his superhuman strength to prevent natural disasters from devastating the region – lifting fallen trees from roads during storms, reinforcing collapsing barns, and rescuing people stranded in harsh weather. His invulnerability allowed him to take on dangerous tasks that would have been impossible for others, like handling runaway livestock or dismantling hazardous machinery without fear of injury.

Even upon gaining his remarkable abilities, Alex remained deeply connected to his roots. He continued to run the ranch, using his strength to maintain the land and care for his animals. His dual life as both a rancher and a superhuman allowed him to bridge the gap between his ordinary world and the extraordinary demands of heroism. He used his platform to promote sustainable farming practices and advocate for the importance of community and mutual support.

Steelheart faced his share of challenges, from people trying to figure out his true identity to adversaries who questioned his motives. Yet, through it all, Alex stayed true to his values. He was driven by a deep sense of duty to his community, embodying the spirit of the land he loved. His unexpected reaction to Vax-23 became a symbol of how one man's quiet resilience and dedication could transform into something far greater than he ever imagined.

Despite the scrutiny and occasional hostility, Alex's commitment to his community never wavered. He continued to use his extraordinary abilities to address not just immediate crises but also to foster long-term resilience and unity. Whether it was aiding in disaster recovery, advocating for sustainable practices, or supporting local initiatives, Steelheart became a pillar of strength and hope.

His efforts inspired others to rally around causes greater than themselves, leading to a revitalized spirit within and around Custer. The challenges he faced only reinforced his resolve, turning him into a symbol of how extraordinary circumstances could bring out the best in humanity. As Alex looked out over his ranch, now thriving once again thanks to his tireless efforts and the support of his community, he realized that his journey was not just about wielding power but about harnessing it to uplift those around him and forge a legacy rooted in courage, compassion, and unwavering dedication.

8
Sylvia

ChronoSpectra

S ylvia Marquez grew up in the vibrant and diverse city of Los Angeles, where her early life was
shaped by a rich cultural tapestry. Born to a Mexi-
can-American family with deep roots in both the ancient and modern worlds, Sylvia was raised with stories
of her ancestors' resilience and the wonders of ancient
civilizations. Her parents, both educators, instilled in
her a profound appreciation for history and the mysteries of the past.

Since she was young, Sylvia was captivated by tales
of lost cities and forgotten artifacts. Her father, a his-

tory professor, would regale her with stories about the
Maya, the Aztecs, and other great civilizations, while
her mother, an artist, nurtured Sylvia's creativity with
vivid depictions of these cultures. This combination of
history and art kindled a passion in Sylvia for anthropology and archaeology.

Academic excellence came naturally to Sylvia. She
excelled in her studies, showing particular aptitude in
anthropology and archaeology. Her inquisitive nature
and dedication earned her a scholarship to study at
an esteemed university, where she pursued her dreams
with fervor. Sylvia's undergraduate years were marked
by fieldwork in various parts of Latin America, where
she uncovered and documented ancient sites, earning
respect and recognition from her peers.

Upon completing her Master's degree, Sylvia em-
barked on a promising academic career. Her research
focused on the influence of ancient cultures on modern
societies, and her innovative approaches soon made her
a leading figure in her field. Despite her success, Sylvia
remained deeply committed to fieldwork, driven by a
desire to experience history firsthand.

In the bustling city of Los Angeles, Sylvia Marquez
was renowned not just for her groundbreaking work
in anthropology but also for her unyielding curiosity
about the world's hidden layers. However, her life took a

dramatic turn during the shutdowns of the V-23 virus. Universities were hit hard, completely halting studies as the virus broke out. As an educator, Sylvia was the first in line to receive the new Vax-23 shot. She was ready to return to work and excited about the new marvels the vaccine promised to humanity. Sylvia, always a staunch advocate for science and public health, received the vaccine without hesitation. She never imagined that this seemingly ordinary action would alter her life in unimaginable ways.

The vaccine, publicized as a marvel of modern science, was supposed to be a simple precaution. However, Sylvia's experience was anything but ordinary. Within hours of receiving the shot, she noticed peculiar changes. At first, it was small things: a fleeting blur in her peripheral vision, objects seeming to shift slightly out of focus. However, as the days went by, the changes became more pronounced. She discovered she could move with incredible speed – so fast that the world around her seemed to freeze, and she could easily dodge obstacles or traverse entire city blocks in mere seconds. Overwhelmed and uncertain at first, Sylvia began to experiment with her newfound powers, driven by her insatiable curiosity and scientific rigor. She had always been fascinated by the intricacies of human behavior and cultural practices.

One afternoon, as she navigated the bustling streets of the city on her way home from work, her mind was deep in thought about the latest adverse reactions from what appeared to be related to Vax-23. Suddenly, the blaring horn of an approaching car jolted her back to reality. Time seemed to slow as she instinctively leaped to the side, but instead of just dodging the vehicle, she found herself standing on the opposite side of the street, a good ten feet away from where she had just been.

Disoriented, Sylvia blinked, her heart racing as she processed what had just happened. "Did I just teleport?" The surrounding environment felt both familiar and surreal, like a dream where the laws of physics no longer applied. As she stood there, trying to comprehend her newfound abilities, a thrill coursed through her veins. Was this some sort of phenomenon? Soon, the realization settled in: Vax-23. Sylvia's mind raced with possibilities as she thought, "Was this also an effect of the vaccine?"

Sylvia soon realized that she could teleport, disappearing from one location and reappearing in another with just a thought. The side effects of the vaccine had unlocked extraordinary abilities that defied the boundaries of her former life.

Ever the scientist and scholar, Sylvia initially approached her newfound powers with a mix of skepticism and excitement. Her anthropological mind raced with questions: Were these powers a result of genetic alterations? Had the vaccine somehow activated latent abilities within her? Driven by her scientific curiosity, she began to study her powers with the same meticulous attention she had once reserved for ancient texts and artifacts.

As she delved into the nature of her abilities, Sylvia started to see them as more than just curiosities. Her super speed and teleportation allowed her to access and study distant, remote, or otherwise inaccessible sites and artifacts in record time. She visited lost ruins in the heart of dense jungles, ancient temples buried beneath deserts, or submerged relics in the depths of the ocean – all within a matter of hours. She could now explore and document distant and dangerous archaeological sites in record time, uncovering artifacts and information that had previously been out of reach. Sylvia used her powers to access and preserve ancient relics, often operating under the radar to avoid disrupting the delicate balance of these historical sites. Her work revolutionized the field of anthropology as she gathered data and artifacts that had previously been inaccessible for decades.

With great power, Sylvia knew she had to be cautious. Her abilities could easily lead to unintended consequences if used recklessly. She decided she would call her new persona "ChronoSpectra." A name that reflects her unique ability to navigate both time and space with incredible speed and precision, as well as her deep connection to history and the past. "Chrono" signifies her command over time, while "Spectra" hints at her ability to appear and disappear in the blink of an eye, much like a spectral presence moving through the ages.

ChronoSpectra meticulously planned each journey she went on, ensuring that her interventions did not disturb the delicate balance of historical sites. Her super speed allowed her to avoid detection and interference, while her teleportation helped her navigate treacherous or restricted areas with ease.

Sylvia's cautious approach was also driven by her acute awareness of the potential for her powers to attract unwanted attention. Government agencies and other powerful organizations would likely take quick notice of her extraordinary abilities, recognizing the tremendous benefits and significant risks. There were constant thoughts of covert operations and clandestine interests who may be eager to harness her super speed and teleportation for their own agendas, from espionage to rapid response missions. Sylvia did not want any involvement in high-stakes projects or elite teams, she remained wary. She knew that her abilities, if exploited or controlled by those with ulterior motives, could lead to dangerous manipulations of historical narratives or jeopardize the very sites she sought to protect. The challenge was not only to use her powers responsibly but also to guard against those who might seek to turn her extraordinary capabilities to serve their own ends, undermining her mission to preserve the truth of the past.

Despite the thrill of her newfound powers, Sylvia remained grounded by her upbringing and values. She approached her superhero responsibilities with the same dedication and integrity she had shown in her academic career. Her missions were guided by a commitment to preserving history and a respect for the cultures she studied. To safeguard the delicate balance between her extraordinary abilities and her scholarly pursuits, Sylvia kept her powers a closely guarded secret. By concealing her abilities from the public eye, she ensured that her work would be evaluated on its merits rather than overshadowed by sensationalism or misconceptions. This secrecy allowed her to operate freely and effectively while protecting both her mission and the sensitive contexts in which she worked.

9

A Convergence
of Heroes

Mark, Elena, Lydia, Alex, and Sylvia all spent the next few months attempting to adjust to their new lives. Each had discovered a new persona, but felt alone in their search for answers as to why they were experiencing such effects, and if anyone else had as well. The country was in disarray, the government corrupt and untrustworthy, and individuals all seemed to be in survival mode as the country – and world – appeared to struggle to recover from the outbreak, shutdown, and the experimental Vax-23 distribution. Vaccine injuries were now being acknowledged in the news, but there was no discussion of anyone who experienced superhuman effects.

The ImmunoCare Foundation was making headlines as an attempt for people to have some recognition of the Vax-23 impact. ImmunoCare operated as a non-profit organization dedicated to providing financial assistance, medical support, and advocacy for individuals who experienced adverse reactions to vaccines. It aimed to bridge the gap between victims and the resources they need for treatment, recovery, and rehabilitation. The Foundation also worked to raise awareness about vaccine injuries, promote research for safer vaccination practices, and support legislation that ensures fair treatment and compensation for affected individuals.

In particular, the most recent headlines were focused on the ImmunoCare Summit & Benefit Gala. A premier national event hosted by the ImmunoCare Foundation to raise awareness, gather support, and provide crucial funding for individuals affected by vaccine injuries. This dual-purpose event combined a high-profile summit with a glamorous gala, bringing together medical professionals, policymakers, survivors, advocates, and the general public. Unbeknownst to each other, all five individuals, among millions of others, had received invitations to attend.

The day the invitations arrived was an ordinary one, but for these five people scattered across the country, it marked the beginning of an extraordinary journey. Each envelope, adorned with the emblem of the ImmunoCare Foundation, held the promise of change and connection.

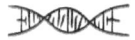

Mark sat in his small, cluttered office, the hum of his old air conditioner barely masking the soft jingle of the mail slot. The letter landed on his desk amidst a pile of invoices and receipts. His eyes, weary from long hours managing his projects, widened as he saw the elegant seal. He had been advocating for vaccine safety since he had suffered a severe adverse reaction. The invitation was a beacon of hope, a chance to connect with others who had walked a similar path. Mark carefully opened the envelope and read the details, his heart thudding with a mix of excitement and nervous anticipation. The ImmunoCare Summit & Benefit Gala promised not just an opportunity to gain support but to stand alongside people who may understand his struggle.

Elena was in the midst of reviewing the latest data from a public health research article when she noticed the envelope in the stack of mail on her desk. Its refined appearance a stark contrast to the paperwork scattered across her workspace. As a dedicated EMT with a newfound focus on vaccine safety, Elena had recently become a vocal advocate for more rigorous safety protocols. The gala was a significant event, bringing together experts and advocates in a shared cause. Her mind raced with thoughts of potential collaborations and breakthroughs. The invitation felt like a validation of the hard work she had put in for her community, as well as a chance to push the boundaries of research into new realms of impact – including superhuman effects.

Lydia unfolded the letter her parents had handed her in their living room. After Lydia had lost her research position and suffered from her own vaccine reaction, she poured herself into support groups and advocacy. The gala was a glimmer of hope, a space where her voice might be amplified and her efforts recognized. She imagined meeting others who had experienced the same pain, and perhaps finding new avenues to advocate for others like herself. The invitation was a sign that her struggles had not gone unnoticed and that there was a larger community ready to stand together.

Alex received his invitation while sifting through a stack of mail at his kitchen table. The envelope, pristine and formal, stood out against the backdrop of his old ranch house. Alex had seen the challenges faced by Vax-23 firsthand, struggling to adjust to his new dual life. The gala was more than a networking opportunity, it was a chance to deepen his understanding of the issues he faced and maybe connect with fellow individuals committed to addressing them. The event promised to be a convergence of expertise and advocacy, a platform where insights could find new purpose and direction.

Sylvia opened the envelope inside her small office at school, surrounded by flyers and posters for various local events. As a community organizer working tirelessly to raise awareness about vaccine injuries in underserved areas, Sylvia saw the gala as a pivotal moment. It was a chance to connect with national figures and potential allies who could help amplify her grassroots efforts. The invitation felt like a validation of her work and an opportunity to bring new resources and support to her community. She envisioned the gala as a stage where her advocacy could gain new momentum and her voice could join a chorus of change.

As the date of the ImmunoCare Summit & Benefit Gala drew near, Mark, Elena, Lydia, Alex, and Sylvia each prepared for their journey to the event. Their paths had yet to cross, but their shared commitment to addressing vaccine injuries, and their search for others who may have experienced superhuman side effects created a common bond that would soon bring them together. Each one had their own story, their own reason for attending – the gala promised to be a place where their individual struggles and achievements could converge into something greater.

10
The Gala

Anticipation grew as they prepared for the event –
a sense of both excitement and trepidation. The gala
would be more than a gathering; it would be a turning
point, where their collective efforts could begin to shape
the future of vaccine safety and support for those affected. ImmunoCare knew that this was more than just an
invitation. It was the start of something meaningful, a
chance to unite their voices and make a lasting impact.

Michigan Stadium, nicknamed "The Big House," is
one of the largest stadiums in the world, and was selected for this reason to host the Gala. The football arena is
located at the University of Michigan in Ann Arbor. The
number of attendees was unknown, many were invited.
The goal: allow as many as possible to attend in an effort
to raise more awareness and enable a larger community
connection.

The day was full of events: lectures, group meetings,
and keynotes from other organizations. There were over
100,000 in attendance for sure. People spoke about

vaccine injuries and deaths of loved ones, all impacts
on life from many walks of life. It was inspiring to see
so many come together, but also scary. Scary so many
had suffered from what was supposed to be a safe solution to the V-23 virus. "I cannot believe there are this
many people here who have suffered," Mark thought to
himself. "Still, I am unsure how many have experienced
superhuman side effects like myself..." He had mingled
with many, but throughout the day, he was unable to
identify any that may have endured a reaction similar to
his own.

The evening air was crisp, a refreshing contrast to
the warmth of the bustling Michigan Stadium where
the ImmuoCare Gala was in full swing. The iconic
bowl, usually echoing with cheers from football fans,
was transformed into a glittering venue, illuminated
by strings of twinkling lights and adorned with lush
floral arrangements. Each detail had been meticulously
planned to create an atmosphere of elegance and hope,
a fitting homage to the organization's mission of raising
awareness about vaccine injuries.

Mark stood at the edge of the field, his hands tucked
deep into his pockets, feeling the gentle hum around
him. He wore a tailored navy suit that highlighted his
tall, lean frame, but despite his polished appearance,
unease flickered in his dark eyes. The gala was an op-

portunity to connect with like-minded individuals, yet he felt like an interloper in this sea of laughter and lively chatter. The stories he carried, tales of heartbreak and loss, felt heavy on his shoulders.

"Beautiful, isn't it?" A voice broke through his reverie.

Mark turned to see a woman with wavy chestnut hair cascading down her shoulders, her bright green eyes sparkling like the lights above. She wore a flowing emerald gown that danced around her as she moved. "I'm Elena," she introduced herself, extending a hand. "I've been following ImmuoCare and it's outreach. I think they've done a great job as a host today."

"Mark," he replied, shaking her hand and feeling a surprising warmth in her grip. "I'm new to the organization."

"New, but passionate, I can tell," she smiled, glancing toward the stage where the evening's keynote speaker, a well-known activist, was preparing to take the mic. "You'll find your people here. This community is special."

As they spoke, the sounds of laughter and chatter began to blur into a distant hum. Mark felt an unexpected sense of belonging, a flicker of connection that he hadn't anticipated. Just then, a commotion near the entrance caught his attention. A woman in a striking red dress entered, her presence commanding and magnetic.

"That's Lydia," Elena whispered, her voice low with awe. "She's been pivotal in advocacy efforts."

Mark watched as Lydia, her hair a waterfall of light curls, engaged with several attendees, her confidence radiating as she passionately shared her story. He admired how she moved through the crowd, her voice carrying a blend of authority and empathy. Just a few feet away, a man with tousled dark hair and a rough look joined the conversation.

"Who's that?" Mark asked, curious.

"I met him earlier, his name is Alex," Elena replied, her eyes softening. "He's a rancher and has seen the other side of vaccine injuries. He seems a bit out of place at an event like this, but I can see he has good intentions."

"Sounds compelling," Mark said, nodding.

As the evening progressed, the crowd began to shift, drawing closer to the stage. The keynote address was about to begin, and a wave of anticipation rippled through the air. Mark felt a pull toward the front but hesitated, unsure if he belonged in such a spotlight. Just then, a petite woman with short dark hair and round glasses approached him.

"Excuse me," she said, her voice soft yet confident. "Is this seat taken?"

"Help yourself," Mark replied. "I'm Mark."

"Sylvia," she said, extending her hand. "I'm an advocate for transparency in vaccine safety. It's a privilege to meet you."

He shook her hand, intrigued by her earnestness. "What's your connection to the organization?"

"I have been impacted by a vaccine injury," she said, her voice steady despite the weight of her words. "I want to make sure no one else has to go through what I have experienced."

Mark's heart sank, empathy flooding through him. He had met too many with similar stories, their pain raw and palpable. "I'm so sorry," he managed, sincerity etched across his face. "Thank you for sharing."

Elena, sitting next to Mark, joined them, her smile fading as she listened. "Sylvia, you should meet Lydia and Alex. They're both incredible advocates."

At that moment, Lydia and Alex approached, their animated discussion momentarily interrupted by the group's presence. "What are you all talking about?" Lydia inquired, her keen eyes flitting between them.

"Mark and Sylvia, both here as vaccine injury advocates," Elena explained.

"Glad to have you, Mark and Sylvia," Lydia said warmly, extending a hand. "This is the place to be if you want to make a difference."

Alex chimed in, "We're all in this together, right? Every voice counts." He grinned, his demeanor was heavy but still, he put forth an effort to put everyone at ease. "It's not just about advocacy; it's about community. We've got to lift each other."

As the lights dimmed and the crowd hushed for the keynote speaker, Mark felt a sudden rush of hope. He looked around at the five of them gathered beneath the glimmering lights, and at that moment, he understood they were no longer strangers. Each of them carried a piece of the same struggle, threads of their stories woven together by shared experiences of pain and resilience. Even more, he couldn't shake the feeling that they may also be searching for others who have experienced something more. He couldn't explain why he felt this, but suddenly, he seemed to have found himself for the first time since the vaccine turned his life upside down.

The speaker took the stage and as her voice filled the stadium, Mark felt an electric charge in the air. It wasn't just the passion in her words, it was the realization that he had finally found a space where they could be heard, a community that welcomed the truth.

As the speech progressed, the group remained close, exchanging glances and nods of agreement. Each of them had arrived carrying their own burdens, but now, they were united in their mission. After the speaker finished, applause erupted like a wave and Mark caught Lydia's eye.

"Let's talk more about how we can make an impact," she said, her enthusiasm infectious.

Sylvia nodded, her eyes bright with determination. "Yes, we need to share our stories, make sure people know they're not alone."

Elena added, "The more we connect, the stronger our voices become. Let's strategize tonight."

Mark's heart swelled as he listened to them. This had become more than just a gala; it was the beginning of something profound. He had entered the stadium feeling isolated, but now he stood amidst a group of possible allies. People are ready to fight for the truth. Beneath the bright lights of Michigan Stadium, surrounded by newfound friends, he felt hope flickering to life – a promise that together, they could spark change.

11

Camaraderie

As the applause faded and the gala drew to a close, the group of five lingered at the edge of the field, exchanging opinions about the evening's speeches. The stadium lights, still shimmering above them, seemed to amplify their burgeoning camaraderie.

"Who's up for grabbing a drink?" Alex suggested, his eyes bright under the brim of his hat. "I know a great little bar nearby where we can unwind and talk more."

Mark felt a surge of gratitude. After the emotional weight of the evening, the thought of continuing the conversation in a more relaxed setting was comforting. "I'm in," he said, glancing around to gauge everyone else's response.

"Absolutely," Elena chimed in, tucking a loose strand of hair behind her ear. "I'd love to hear more about your experiences, Mark."

Sylvia nodded, a soft smile crossing her face. "I'd like that too. It's nice to be with people who understand."

Lydia crossed her arms, a thoughtful look on her face. "Let's do it. We need to connect more, share our stories – it'll help us all feel less alone."

With that, they made their way out of the stadium, the cool evening air refreshing after the warmth of the gala. They walked in a loose formation, laughter mingling with the distant sounds of the city as they headed to a nearby pub, its neon sign flickering invitingly.

Inside, the ambiance was cozy, with wooden beams and low-hanging lights creating a warm glow. They settled around a round table, the clinking of glasses and the soft hum of conversations providing a comfortable backdrop. Mark felt a wave of relief wash over him; this was a different kind of gathering – one filled with understanding.

As they placed their drink orders, Lydia leaned forward, her eyes sparkling with curiosity. "So, Mark, why did you get involved with ImmuoCare? What's your story?"

Taking a deep breath, Mark glanced at each of them, feeling a sense of safety in their presence. "I was an advocate for the vaccine, mostly so I could return to work. I am an engineer, the shutdown was hard on progress.

Once Vax-23 was released, I was eager to receive it and return to normal life. However, I experienced some rare side effects and work did not return to normal... instead, my whole life shifted completely. I felt compelled to speak out, to raise awareness about the risks that some may face. It has cost me a lot – family, friends, colleagues... It's been a lonely path."

Sylvia listened intently, her expression sympathetic. "I can relate. Facing my own injuries, I felt like I was shouting into a void. People didn't want to hear it; they'd rather stick to their narratives. I, too, have felt alone in my experience."

"It's unfair that you – we – have had to bear that alone," Mark replied, his voice steady but filled with compassion.

"Thank you," Sylvia said, her eyes glistening with unshed tears. "I've learned to channel that pain into advocacy. I want to prevent others from experiencing what I have."

The group shared a moment of silence, each of them processing the weight of her words. Alex broke the tension. "This is why it's so important to have spaces like this, we need to uplift each other. 'Lonely' is a good word to describe what I have gone through as well. My side effects also seem to be unheard of, I have yet to meet another who shares what I have been through."

"It's strange, no one has said what symptoms they have actually experienced – and no one has asked... could they also be superhuman?" Lydia thought to herself. Elena interrupted her thoughts by raising her glass and stating, "To community. To finding strength in our shared experiences."

They clinked their glasses together, the sound ringing out like a promise. As the drinks flowed, so did their stories.

Elena shared her journey as an activist, recounting her experiences lobbying for vaccine safety legislation. "It's exhausting," she admitted, "but every small victory makes it worth it. When I see someone feel empowered to speak out, it reminds me why I do this."

Mark nodded in agreement. "It's a ripple effect. Every conversation, every person we educate can lead to real change."

Lydia leaned in, her voice hesitant, "...that's why we need to be bold. People often shy away from the topic, but silence only allows misinformation to thrive."

As they spoke, the laughter and chatter in the bar created a comforting atmosphere, yet the gravity of their conversations brought an intensity that kept their focus sharp. Mark felt the burden of his past experiences lightening with each story, a shared catharsis unfolding at their table.

After a round of drinks, Alex leaned back in his chair, a thoughtful expression crossing his face. "What's the biggest challenge you all face? Mine has been finding ways to break through the noise. People often switch off when they hear anything vaccine-related."

"That's exactly it," Lydia said, nodding vigorously. "There's so much misinformation out there that it feels like we're fighting an uphill battle. We need strategies that resonate with everyday people."

"Connecting on a human level is crucial," Sylvia added, her voice firm. "When I tell my story, it's not just statistics; it's a life that was changed forever. If we can make it personal, maybe we can reach more hearts."

Mark felt a swell of determination. "Maybe we can create resources together, something that combines our strengths."

Elena's eyes lit up. "That's brilliant! If we can create a safe space for dialogue, we can start bridging that gap. We need to normalize these conversations."

The table buzzed with energy, each person bouncing ideas off one another, the possibilities feeling almost tangible. They began sketching out a plan on napkins, scribbling notes about a potential future they could share. As the clock ticked toward midnight, the bar's atmosphere shifted from lively chatter to a more subdued backdrop, but their enthusiasm remained undiminished.

Finally, as the last round of drinks was served, Sylvia glanced at her watch. "I hate to break this up, but we should probably wrap up soon. I've got an early morning."

Mark looked around at his new friends, a sense of bitter-sweetness settling in. "I'm really glad we did this. It feels good to talk openly, to share."

"Absolutely," Lydia replied, her eyes bright. "We should make this a regular thing. Support each other, brainstorm, and keep this momentum going."

As they rose to leave, Elena took out her phone. "Let's exchange contact information. We can set up another meeting, maybe plan some sort of get-together."

They huddled close, fingers tapping on screens, the air filled with a buzz of excitement. Mark saved each contact, feeling a sense of warmth wash over him with every name he added.

"Let's do this again soon," he said, looking around at each of their faces, now familiar and encouraging.

"Definitely," Alex agreed. "We'll keep the momentum going and make sure our voices are heard."

With their plans solidified, they stepped out into the cool night air, the city lights twinkling around them. Mark felt a warmth spread through him, buoyed by the connection they had forged. The journey ahead would undoubtedly be challenging, however, he felt equipped to face it for the first time – no longer alone, surrounded by allies ready to advocate for change.

As they parted ways, each of them carried the spark of hope ignited that night, ready to fan the flames of their collective mission.

12

Unmasking Truths

A month had passed since that fated night at the bar, and the group had maintained a steady stream of communication, their digital conversations weaving together plans, ideas, and encouragement. They shared articles, debated strategies, and even collaborated on a draft for a community workshop raising Vax-23 injury awareness. The camaraderie they had formed was both unexpected and invigorating, and they found themselves anticipating their next gathering.

Finally, they settled on a date for an in-person meeting in Montana at Glacier National Park. They all lived in different states across the country, a trip to Glacier sounded relaxing and agreed upon as a good location to meet. They agreed to meet at a café outside the park the morning after they all arrived. The café, with its rustic charm and eclectic decor, felt like the perfect setting for the revelations they were about to share. As

Mark entered, the rich aroma of coffee enveloped him, mingling with the low hum of conversation. He spotted Lydia already seated at a corner table, her bouncy hair glowing under the soft light.

"Hey, Mark!" she called, waving him over. "Glad you could make it!"

"Wouldn't miss it," he replied, sliding into the chair across from her. "How have you been?"

"Busy, but good! I've been brainstorming some ideas for our group," she said, her excitement evident. "I think we could really make a difference."

One by one, the others arrived: Elena, her confidence radiating as she took a seat next to Lydia; Alex, his broad smile infectious; and finally Sylvia, her energy palpable as she strolled into the café. They all exchanged greetings, the familiarity of their recent interactions making it feel more like a reunion than a meeting.

After placing their orders, they settled in, the conversation flowing effortlessly. They discussed their individual progress since the gala, sharing small victories and challenges in their advocacy efforts.

Then, as the coffee arrived and steam curled into the air, Lydia leaned forward, her expression suddenly serious. "I think we should talk about something important today. Really important."

Mark raised an eyebrow, sensing the energy shift. "What do you mean?"

"Remember when we shared our stories about our vaccine experiences? I think it's time we reveal another layer of ourselves," she whispered, glancing at the others for support.

"Okay, I'm intrigued," Elena said, leaning in. "What's on your mind?"

"It's about... abilities," Lydia continued, her voice low. "I think we all know we're not just ordinary people anymore. The vaccines did something to us, didn't they? Something extraordinary."

Mark's heart raced. He had felt different ever since that momentous day at the gala, but he hadn't dared to acknowledge it fully. "Are you suggesting what I think you are?"

"Exactly," Lydia replied, her eyes sparkling. Suddenly, a spoon rose and hovered just a few inches over the table, bent in half, and gently lowered back down. "I've been able to do things I can't explain – things I've only seen in movies. I have telepathy, telekinesis, even a kind of mental healing, and that's just the beginning."

The table went silent as they processed the spoon bending and her words. Lydia was beginning to feel vulnerable, maybe she misread the group and shouldn't have exposed herself. Just then, Mark took a breath, feeling a mix of disbelief and relief. "I've noticed changes too. I can manipulate energy at a quantum level – force fields, energy blasts... even reshaping my surroundings." He wrapped his hands around his cup and it suddenly began to boil, as if it was being reheated on a stove.

Elena's eyes widened, she felt a surge of bravery after their confessions. The shadow from the sugar container sitting on the table began to dance around across the tabletop as if the sun was quickly spinning around them. "I can manipulate shadows and darkness. I can traverse through them, become unseen. It's like I can control the very fabric of night."

"Wow!" Alex interrupted, clearly impressed. He suddenly took a knife and ran the blade across the palm of his hand. To their astonishment, he didn't bleed – no mark was left. "I thought I was alone in this. I've developed incredible strength and my skin feels impenetrable. It's like I can withstand anything thrown my way."

Sylvia nodded eagerly, her hands animated as she spoke. "I've got super speed – like I'm running on a different plane of existence. I can even teleport. It feels unreal!" Suddenly, she was waving from the other side of the café. Not one person had witnessed her movements from the table to the drink station nestled in the corner.

As Sylvia sat back down, Mark looked around the table, awe and excitement coursing through him. "So, we're superheroes?"

"Seems that way," Lydia grinned. "I have done a ton of research on this following the trials I was fired from after the development of my own abilities. It's like we've been given these powers as a side effect of the vaccine. It's wild!"

"I knew it!" Alex blurted.

Mark let out a laugh as he felt relieved he wasn't alone. They all began to laugh, the tension dissipating as the realization settled in that they shared such experiences. The enormity of their newfound identities began to unfold, and Mark felt a sense of unity enveloping them. This was no longer just about vaccine advocacy; they were now part of something larger.

"Imagine what we could do together," Sylvia said in a hushed voice tinged with excitement. "We could raise awareness and protect those who feel vulnerable in this space.

"Think about it," Elena added. "Maybe we could host workshops and demonstrations to showcase not just our advocacy, but our abilities as well. We can engage the community in a way they've never seen before."

Mark's mind raced with possibilities. "We could create a coalition. We'd be the face of change."

"Absolutely!" Lydia replied, enthusiasm bubbling over. "Let's not just be advocates; let's be superheroes for this cause."

They spent the next hour brainstorming ideas, each suggestion building upon the last. The group had left the café for fear of being overheard and were now in the park. The beauty around them faded into the background as they envisioned what they were capable of when they combined their powers with their advocacy.

As their conversation deepened, a darker current began to surface. Lydia leaned back against a rock, her expression turning serious. "What if we use our powers for something bigger? Something that addresses the root of the issues we're fighting against? The corruption in the healthcare system and the government that often turns a blind eye to the truth?"

"What do you mean?" Mark asked, his interest piqued.

"We've seen how the system protects its own," she continued, her voice steady. "Corporations prioritize profits over people. The government often seems complicit, perpetuating a cycle of misinformation. What if we formed a coalition that not only advocates for change but actively works to dismantle the corrupt structures holding us back?"

Elena nodded, her eyes brightening with the idea. "We could call ourselves the Vanguard Coalition. We'd be the front-line defenders of truth, using our powers to protect those who have been silenced."

"I love it," Sylvia said, leaning forward, her excitement appreciable. "We could engage in strategic actions, raise awareness about the injustices, and even expose those responsible for the misinformation and harm."

Alex crossed his arms, a thoughtful expression on his face. "We need to be careful. We can't put ourselves in unnecessary danger. We must be tactical about this."

Mark felt a fire ignite within him. "I agree, tactical and safe are important. Still, no more silence. We've been given these abilities for a reason. It's time we stand up not just for ourselves, but for everyone who feels powerless in this system. We can blend our activism with direct action, holding those in power accountable."

The group buzzed with energy as they laid the groundwork for their new mission. They hiked through the park as they spoke of strategies, potential targets, and how they could utilize their unique powers to expose the truth. Mark shared his ability to create force fields, envisioning protective barriers around peaceful protests. Lydia imagined using her telepathy to gather intel and inspire unity among activists. Elena pictured navigating through shadows to gather information undetected.

After hours of brainstorming, they began to coalesce around the idea of not only raising awareness but actively working against the corruption that perpetuated harm. They decided to schedule another meeting to plan their first steps. This wouldn't be a one-off effort, but the beginning of a long-term commitment to change.

The evening light began to fade and they headed back to their rental car, energized and filled with purpose. Mark felt a profound sense of belonging; these were not just allies but a family forged in the fires of struggle and hope.

"Let's meet again tomorrow to plan everything out," Mark suggested, feeling a spark of determination.

"We can have breakfast together and then go for another hike," Sylvia said, her eyes shining.

"Can't wait to see what we come up with," Alex grinned.

As they stepped out of the vehicle into the light of the hotel sign, laughter and chatter spilled from the group. Together, they walked into the future as superheroes united not just by their powers, but by their shared commitment to making a difference. With their identities unveiled to one another and their mission clear, they felt unstoppable.

The Vanguard Coalition was born that day, and as they ventured out into the world, they knew they were

ready to take on the challenges ahead. With the government's corruption looming like a shadow, they vowed to
be the light; champions for the voiceless, and warriors
for justice.

13

The Genesis of Vanguard

During their weekend trip to Glacier, Mark had offered his place in Avondale as the next location to meet. He owned private property in the desert that was surrounded by undeveloped acreage with a large underground bunker. The bunker had been built before he had purchased the property. Mark utilized it as a storage space for years, but after that trip, he came back with a new energy to restore it and use it as a meeting space for Vanguard.

The sun dipped below the horizon, casting long shadows over the Arizona desert as Mark prepared for the first official meeting of the Vanguard Coalition. His underground bunker, hidden beneath a modest home on the outskirts of Avondale, was the perfect refuge – equipped with technology, supplies, and a sense of secrecy that felt essential for their mission.

As he descended the stairs into the cool, dimly lit space, anticipation swirled within him. The walls were lined with maps and blueprints, pinned notes of ideas, and strategic plans. A central table surrounded by sturdy chairs awaited his team. He made a final check on the gadgets he'd set up: a projector for presentations, a whiteboard for brainstorming, and an array of monitors displaying news and social media feeds.

Mark had sent a group message earlier, providing directions to his home in a welcome text. The four others had flown in, meeting at the airport with the plan to drive together to his place. As he adjusted the settings on the projector, the sound of footsteps echoed through the bunker announcing his teammates' arrival.

"Wow, Mark, this place is incredible!" Sylvia exclaimed as she stepped inside, her eyes wide with wonder. "I can't believe you put this together for us!"

"It's a work in progress," he replied with a hint of pride in his voice. "Treat it as a second home – it's our base of operations now."

"Base of operations! I like the sound of that," Lydia grinned, taking in the surroundings. "We are really going all in, aren't we?"

"Absolutely," Mark said, feeling the weight of their commitment settle in. "We need a place where we can plan and strategize without the worry of prying eyes."

Elena, her usual energy amplified by the significance of the moment, elatedly added, "I've been looking forward to this since Glacier! I can't wait to see what we come up with together."

Alex arrived last, his demeanor a mix of excitement and seriousness. "So, what's the agenda for our first official meeting?" he asked, glancing around the bunker with a mix of admiration and curiosity.

"Let's gather around," Mark said, motioning to the table. "I want to go over some priorities I've outlined. After that, we can discuss our first steps as the Vanguard Coalition."

They took their seats, the atmosphere charged with anticipation. Mark activated the projector, displaying their mission statement on the screen.

The Vanguard Coalition is a clandestine organization established to challenge the corrupt elements within the U.S. government and powerful corporate entities that manipulate global events for their own benefit. This coalition is driven by the shared goal of exposing corruption, ensuring transparency, and creating a new societal framework based on justice and equity.

Mission and Objectives

1. *Expose Corruption*: The Vanguard Coalition aims to reveal the hidden agendas and corrupt practices

of government officials and corporations. Their mission includes gathering evidence of illicit activities, leaking sensitive information to the public, and holding those in power accountable.

2. *Rescue and Protect*: The coalition is committed to protecting innocent lives caught in the crossfire of political and corporate conflicts. They focus on rescuing individuals who are being exploited or endangered by the government's or corporations' schemes.

3. *Reform and Rebuild*: Beyond just dismantling corrupt systems, the Vanguard Coalition seeks to lay the groundwork for a more transparent, fair, and just society. Their goal is to rebuild societal institutions from the ground up, ensuring that future governance and corporate practices adhere to ethical standards.

"Rebuild the government?" Alex questioned. "I know we are here for advocacy and exposure, but are we really up for this?"

He had a point. This was no small feat, even the gala ImmunoCare hosted was small in comparison.

Elena leaned forward, her eyes glimmering with determination. "I love it. This isn't just about advocating, it's about taking action."

"Exactly," Mark replied, his confidence growing as he spoke. "We need to start by identifying key areas where we can make an impact. We can begin with exposing corruption by leaking evidence – keeping our safety in mind."

Lydia tapped her fingers on the table, her mind racing. "What if we research and gather evidence on Vax-23 and post it online? We could utilize our abilities to gather information... and maybe add information about superhuman side effects. It'll draw attention and spark conversations."

"I like where this is headed," Alex said, nodding. "We need to be strategic. We should target areas with a history of vaccine resistance or misinformation. That's where we can likely make the most significant impact."

Sylvia chimed in, her voice steady. "Social media use can amplify our efforts. If we can go viral, we'll reach a larger audience. We could film some demonstrations as our alter egos and share our stories."

Mark scribbled notes on the whiteboard, capturing their ideas as they flowed. "I think incorporating our personal stories is a good idea. It'll humanize our message and show that we're not just talking about statistics; we're advocating for real people."

After an hour of intense discussion, they had outlined a plan for their first exposé, but as they moved through the agenda, a sense of urgency began to settle.

"Okay, let's talk about the bigger picture," Mark said, looking at each of them. "We've discussed initiatives, but what about going after the corrupt systems themselves? How do we make our voices heard where it matters most?"

Lydia's expression shifted, her usual spark now ignited with intensity. "We need to expose the lies and the people behind them. That means infiltrating some of these organizations – gathering evidence, making connections, and building a case against those who are perpetuating this cycle of misinformation."

Mark felt a chill run down his spine at the weight of their mission. "You're right. We can't just be advocates; we need to be watchdogs, using our powers to uncover the truth."

"We can't put ourselves in danger," Alex cautioned. "We need to strategize our approach carefully."

Sylvia nodded in agreement. "I can use my speed to gather intel quickly and quietly. If I can get in and out without drawing attention, we could collect information that others cannot obtain."

"I can use my shadows to create diversions if needed," Elena added. "We'll have to work together to make sure we're covering each other."

Mark felt a rush of excitement mixed with apprehension. "So, we're all in agreement then? The Vanguard Coalition will not only advocate for change but also actively fight against the corruption we see?"

With solemn nods from everyone, a pact was formed, the gravity of their mission settling over them like a cloak. They weren't just a group of individuals with unique abilities; they were a united front, ready to challenge the status quo.

As they wrapped up the meeting, Lydia suggested they each share what they hoped to achieve through the coalition. Alex spoke of his desire for a future where people felt empowered to make informed decisions. Elena expressed her wish to see transparency in the medical community. Mark wanted to protect those vulnerable to misinformation. Sylvia longed to create a world where no one felt alone in their struggles.

By the end of the night, their resolve was stronger than ever. They had established a bond not just through their powers, but through their shared purpose: a coalition ready to rise against forces that threatened their community and the truth.

While they exited the bunker, stepping back into the crisp Arizona air and the moon glowing over the desert, Mark felt a renewed sense of determination. They were no longer just five individuals fighting for a cause; they were awakened as the Vanguard Coalition, a team poised to make waves in a world desperate for change.

As the stars twinkled above, each one of them thought about how this was just the beginning of their extraordinary journey. Together, they would shine a light on the darkness and fight for a future where truth and justice prevailed.

14
Unveiling Lies

After forming a plan, the group once again broke up to return to their homes. A few weeks had passed before they all flew back out again, this time they had the intention to stay longer. Lydia had committed to moving to the base to help Mark, leaving her parents' house. The others had started to shift their lives to the coalition and were beginning to move out to Arizona, one by one.

The tension in the bunker was palpable as the Vanguard Coalition gathered around the central table, screens illuminating their faces with a flickering blue glow. Mark stood at the head of the table, radiating energy as he prepared for their first real mission – a strategic leak designed to expose the corruption surrounding the controversial experiment, Vax-23.

"Before we dive in," he began, glancing around at his friends and fellow heroes, "let's take a moment to recap how we gathered the information that's about to rock the government's narrative."

Lydia nodded, her eyes sparkling with excitement. "I started with telepathy. I reached out to a few contacts in the medical field – people who had been involved with me in the trials of Vax-23. By establishing a mental link, I could sift through their thoughts, uncovering concerns they hadn't shared publicly."

Mark leaned forward, impressed. "You were able to get direct insight without them realizing it?"

"Exactly. I didn't push too hard; just enough to make them comfortable sharing what they knew. Their fears about the vaccine's rushed approval and potential side effects were illuminating," she replied.

Elena chimed in, "While Lydia was doing that, I used my ability to manipulate shadows to sneak into a few closed-door meetings. It was risky, but I managed to create illusions that kept me hidden. I overheard discussions about suppressing data on adverse reactions and payouts by Biocure, Helix, and MedovaCorp. – information that could change the public's perception of Vax-23."

Mark's heart raced. "That's incredible. The firsthand accounts you gathered will be key to framing our narrative."

Alex, who had been listening intently, added, "I leveraged my strength to access documents from a pharmaceutical facility. I was able to get past a few security measures – just a quick exertion of force, enough to avoid alarms without drawing attention. Those internal memos detailing the financial pressures to push out Vax-23 are invaluable."

Sylvia smiled, her eyes shining with enthusiasm. "I zipped around the city, gathering real-time data from social media and local news. I used my speed to compile statistics on adverse reactions reported online, which helped us understand how widespread the issues are."

Mark surveyed the group, pride swelling in his chest. "We didn't just gather evidence; we formed a comprehensive picture of the situation. Each of you played a crucial role. This is the power of the Vanguard Coalition."

As he spoke, the weight of their mission settled on him. The information they had uncovered was a ticking time bomb, ready to expose the truth about Vax-23 and the shadowy figures behind its rollout.

"Tonight, we're going to change the narrative," he continued, locking eyes with each member of the coalition. "Vax-23 has been touted as a miraculous solution to the V-23 virus for too long. We know the truth is much darker. Our job is to expose that truth and hold those responsible accountable."

Lydia leaned forward, her fingers tapping rhythmically against the table. "We've gathered enough evidence to paint a clear picture. Reports of adverse effects, questionable testing protocols, and evidence of suppression by pharmaceutical companies. This isn't just a rumor; it's a reality that's been hidden from the public."

"Exactly," Mark replied. "Our objective tonight is to leak verified documents and testimonies that outline the corruption behind Vax-23. We'll share everything we have through secure channels to ensure maximum exposure."

Elena's gaze sharpened. "We have to ensure it reaches the right audiences – those who will amplify the message. We can't let it get buried in the noise."

"Agreed," Sylvia said, her voice steady. "I can use my speed and teleportation to gather last-minute information if needed. I'll make sure we have all the data we can find before we hit 'send'."

Mark nodded, feeling a surge of confidence. "Let's finalize our plan. We'll split into teams: Lydia and I will prepare the documents for the leak, while Alex and Elena work on creating a social media strategy to push it out. Sylvia, you'll monitor the conversation online and be ready to jump in if needed."

With their roles assigned, the coalition sprang into action. Mark and Lydia sifted through a mountain of files, identifying key documents that revealed the truth about Vax-23: the troubling data in regard to its financial profit and rushed approval, reports of serious side effects – including deaths – that were purposefully overlooked, and internal communications that showed the government's and various pharmaceutical companies' awareness of potential dangers.

Lydia's eyes widened as she read a particularly damning email. "Listen to this," she said, her voice a mixture of shock and determination. "It's from a lead researcher who expressed concerns about the mRNA technology's long-term effects but was pressured to proceed anyway because of financial incentives. This is gold."

"Perfect," Mark replied, making a note to include it in their leak. "We'll make sure the public sees this."

Meanwhile, Alex and Elena were busy drafting a series of posts designed to grab attention. They focused on creating compelling narratives, weaving in statistics and personal stories from individuals affected by the vaccine. Each post was crafted to evoke emotion and encourage shares, creating a ripple effect that would spread their message far and wide.

"This post will include testimonials from families affected by adverse reactions," Elena suggested, her fingers flying over the keyboard. "It's important we humanize the numbers."

"We should use hashtags strategically," Alex added. "#Vax23Truth, #VaccineSafety, and #ExposingCorruption could help draw in the right audience. We need to ignite a conversation."

Hours slipped by as the team worked seamlessly, fueled by determination and the belief that they could make a difference. Finally, with everything ready, Mark felt the weight of the moment settle on his shoulders.

"Is everyone ready?" he asked, glancing around the table. They all nodded, expressions tired but filled with resolve. "On the count of three, we hit send."

"One... two... three!"

With a collective breath, they pressed the button, launching their carefully curated content into the digital world. Mark's heart raced as he watched the notifications begin to pop up. Comments, shares, and likes surged like a wave crashing on the shore.

Sylvia was already monitoring the online conversation, her eyes darting across multiple screens. "It's quickly gaining traction! People are engaging with the posts, sharing their own experiences. This is it!"

As the conversation began to swell, a darker current emerged. Mark noticed a few comments that were defensive, dismissing their claims as conspiracy theories. His stomach knotted at the thought of the push-back they might face.

"Stay focused," Lydia said, noticing his unease. "We have the truth on our side. The more they push back, the more people will question what's really happening."

The group watched over the next few hours as their posts spread, feeling a mix of exhilaration and anxiety. They knew the risks involved; exposing such information could attract unwanted attention. It was a risk they were willing to take.

Suddenly, Sylvia's voice cut through the tension. "I'm seeing something alarming. There's a wave of coordinated responses against us – accounts with no followers, all posting the same debunking statements. It looks like they're trying to discredit us."

Mark clenched his jaw. "They're scared of us. This means we're hitting a nerve."

"Let's use it to our advantage," Alex suggested. "We can show how these responses are orchestrated, framing it as a desperate attempt to silence dissent. It'll only add to our credibility."

"Perfect," Mark replied, his heart racing with the thrill of the fight. "We can turn their efforts into a weapon for our cause."

The conversation intensified as they strategized their next steps, crafting responses that highlighted the orchestrated attacks while reiterating their message of transparency and truth. As the night wore on, they worked tirelessly, turning their bunker into a hub of activity – voices rising, ideas clashing, and laughter breaking the tension as they found strength in each other.

Outside, the stars twinkled brightly, a silent witness to the storm brewing below ground. The Vanguard Coalition was truly becoming a force for change, ready to take on the shadows of corruption and demand accountability.

As they continued to monitor the growing conversation, Mark felt an undeniable shift in the air. This was just the beginning of the battle. Their efforts would resonate beyond the digital realm, stirring people to question the narrative fed to them. They were standing at the precipice of something monumental.

15

The Fallout

As dawn approached, the coalition members began to feel fatigue creep in, but the adrenaline of their actions kept them energized. Suddenly, Sylvia's eyes widened in alarm as she pointed to her monitor. "Guys, look at this!"

They all leaned in, seeing the comments and posts they had sparked gaining momentum. Troubling was the appearance of higher-profile figures – politicians, news anchors, and even celebrities – beginning to weigh in on the issue.

"This is getting bigger than we anticipated," Lydia said, her voice tinged with excitement and concern. "Look, they're starting to cover our leak on news outlets. This could go national."

As the news of the leak spread, Mark's phone buzzed with a message from a contact he had made during his initial investigations. The message was terse, filled with urgency: "They're panicking. Sources within the government are worried about a coalition they can't identify. They think someone is watching."

Mark shared the message and exchanged glances with the others, their expressions a mixture of fear and resolve. "We've struck a nerve, and now the government is aware of us. They'll want to suppress this."

"We need to stay ahead of them," Alex said, his voice steady. "We can't let them control the narrative. We've done this for the people, and we can't back down now."

They spent the following hours drafting press releases, preparing responses to likely inquiries, and creating backup plans in case they needed to shift their operations. The bunker buzzed with activity, each member focused on their role, fueled by the gravity of their mission.

Meanwhile, high above in the nation's capital, President Walker sat in a dimly lit conference room, surrounded by his advisors. The room was heavy with tension, a stark contrast to the bright morning sun filtering through the windows outside.

"Sir, we have a situation," Angela, said, sliding a stack of printouts across the polished table. "There's a coordinated leak in regard to Vax-23. We believe it is a group identifying as the Vanguard Coalition. They are gaining significant traction online."

The President scanned the documents, his frown deepening with each line he read. "How did this happen? I thought we had everything under control."

"We underestimated their reach and ability to organize," another advisor chimed into the conversation. "The leak includes internal emails, research data, and testimonies from individuals adversely affected by the vaccine. We are unsure as to how they have gathered so much sensitive information. It's compelling."

"What are the implications?" Walker asked, running a hand through his hair, visibly agitated.

"If this continues to spread, it could undermine public trust in the vaccine program and the administration's credibility," Angela replied. "We need to act quickly to mitigate the damage."

"We can't let this get out of hand," Walker said, his voice steady but urgent. "I want all resources focused on identifying this coalition. We need to know who they are, where they are located, and how they're managing to operate without detection."

As the meeting continued, Walker's mind raced with possibilities. This was more than just a public relations issue; it was a threat to their entire agenda. The V-23 virus had already wreaked havoc, and Vax-23 was supposed to be the answer. If this unknown coalition could disrupt that narrative, they would not only challenge his presidency but also the very structure of the health policies he had championed.

The emergence of the Vanguard Coalition as a significant force challenging the status quo of the U.S. government and major corporations triggers a multi-faceted and intense reaction from the government. Their response must involve a complex combination of political maneuvering, security measures, and public relations strategies aimed at undermining and neutralizing the coalition's efforts.

"Tell me, what have we figured out as a reactive plan?" Walker asked, interrupting his own thoughts.

"A public relations campaign," Angela responded, pushing her glasses up the bridge of her nose as she spoke. "It is designed to discredit the Vanguard Coalition. Using media channels, we can portray the coalition as a group of vigilantes and terrorists threatening national security and public safety. We will have them emphasize that the coalition's actions are illegal and pose a danger to innocent civilians in an attempt to sway public opinion against them."

To bolster their narrative, the government spreads misinformation and propaganda, suggesting that the coalition's leaders have ulterior motives and are driven by personal vendettas. They highlight any incidents where the coalition's actions inadvertently caused collateral damage, framing these as evidence of their recklessness.

"We will also ramp up surveillance efforts, employing advanced monitoring technologies and intelligence networks to track the coalition's activities. This includes electronic surveillance, data mining, and the use of drones and other reconnaissance tools to gather information on the coalition's operations. We have to find out where they are located and how they obtained this information," Walker demanded as he slammed his fist on the table.

"Yes, sir. We have already gathered a specialized counter-intelligence team to identify and neutralize informants and potential allies of the coalition. This team will work to infiltrate and disrupt the coalition's communications and logistical support." Angela said, attempting to reassure President Walker that they were ahead of the coalition.

"In response to the coalition's actions, we can initiate legal proceedings against members of the Vanguard Coalition. We will pursue charges of terrorism, sedition, and other serious crimes, aiming to criminalize their activities and dissuade potential supporters." Angela added. "We can utilize high-profile arrests and trials as a tactic to showcase the government's resolve and create fear with the hopes we deter others from joining the cause."

"Screw any trial," Walker said as he threw a pen he had been using to scribble notes. "We need to get them into custody and send them straight to Gitmo. We don't want to give the media a chance to humanize these freaks." He leaned back in his chair, pressing his fingers together under his chin as if he were thinking hard. "We will leverage the public's fear by exaggerating the potential dangers posed by the coalition. Have the news highlight hypothetical scenarios involving widespread chaos and destruction. This will create a justification for us to crack down while we gain public support for our measures."

Walker stood up and pushed his chair back. "If we can use disinformation campaigns to create paranoia and confusion while leveraging psychological manipulation to exploit personal vulnerabilities, we may be able to take this coalition out before it ever gains traction." He walked towards the door. "This will be nothing more than a forgotten viral conspiracy," he smugly said as he left the room, the door slamming behind him.

As the President strategized with his team, the Vanguard Coalition continued to prepare in their bunker, unaware of the impending storm. They were determined to continue to shine a light on the corruption that had tainted the promise of Vax-23. United by their purpose and their unique abilities, they were ready to confront whatever challenges lay ahead.

16

Heroes in Disguise

The bright lights of the news studio illuminated the somber expressions of the anchors seated behind the sleek glass desk. The television screen behind them displayed a bold headline: "Vanguard Coalition: Spreading Misinformation or Heroes in Disguise?"

As the camera zoomed in, anchor Rebecca Lane spoke with a tone that dripped with skepticism. "In recent weeks, the so-called Vanguard Coalition has gained traction online, claiming to expose corruption surrounding the vaccine, Vax-23. We must ask: are they a legitimate force for good, or are they simply spreading false information in an attempt to undermine public trust?"

Her co-anchor, Brian Chen, leaned forward, his voice firm. "The coalition has faced criticism from various government officials, who allege that their claims are unfounded. Many believe this group is leveraging sensationalism involving the safety and efficacy of the V-23 vaccine to cause upheaval against the US government."

As the anchors continued their segment, displaying clips of politicians denouncing the coalition, Mark, Lydia, Elena, Alex, and Sylvia sat in Mark's underground bunker, watching the broadcast with growing frustration.

"This is ridiculous," Sylvia said, her arms crossed. "They're trying to paint us as villains just because we've exposed their secrets."

Mark ran a hand through his hair, his mind racing. "This was to be expected... we need a response. We can't let them control the narrative like this. We've already shown them we're a threat."

Lydia nodded, her expression thoughtful. "How? We can't just release more documents. They'll continue to discredit us. We need to show our legitimacy in a way they can't ignore."

Alex leaned back in his chair, flexing his muscles absently. "Well... what if we showcase our powers? We can speak directly to the people instead of letting the news speak on our behalf. A demonstration of who we are and what we can do. If we show the public that we're not just people behind keyboards, but real heroes, it might change how they perceive us."

Mark's eyes widened. "That could work. If we expose our identities as superheroes – without revealing our personal lives – we could shift the conversation entirely. We'd need to frame it as a response to the lies being spread."

Sylvia perked up, her energy infectious. "We can go live on social media! We can show the public what we're capable of and prove that our powers are adverse reactions to Vax-23. We'll own our narrative."

Lydia's brows furrowed with concern. "What if it backfires? What if they use our powers against us or twist the narrative even more?"

"We'll be prepared," Mark assured her. "We'll focus on our mission – to protect the public and expose the truth. We'll make sure our real identities remain anonymous. It's about the message, not us as individuals."

After a moment of deliberation, the group nodded in agreement. The frustration in the room shifted, transformed by a surge of determination. They had a plan.

An hour later, the team gathered around a camera set up in the bunker, a backdrop of their emblems displayed behind them. Each emblem symbolized their powers and the shared purpose that had brought them together. Mark adjusted the camera, glancing at the others who were wearing outfits and masks to obscure their identities.

"Okay, we're live in three... two... one..."

Mark cleared his throat, his heart pounding. "Hello, everyone. We are the Vanguard Coalition. You may have heard our name in the news recently. We want to take this moment to address the misinformation being spread about us."

Lydia stepped forward, her presence commanding. "We are not here to spread fear or confusion. We are here to share the truth about Vax-23 and its impact on countless individuals. The powers we possess..."

Elena raised her hand, creating a flicker of shadow that danced across the room, swirling like a wisp, as she finished Lydia's sentence: "...are a direct result of the vaccine. Not by our approval, we've been granted abilities, and we're using them to protect you and reveal the truth behind the corruption in our government and the pharmaceutical industry."

Sylvia zipped around the camera in a blur, appearing beside Mark in an instant. "We want to assure you that we are on your side. Our goal is to ensure your safety and well-being. The stories you've heard about us being villains are fabrications designed to distract you from the real issues."

Mark took a deep breath, feeling the weight of their message. "We understand the fear and uncertainty surrounding Vax-23, but we want you to know that we are here to fight for transparency. We are committed to holding those in power accountable."

Suddenly, Alex stepped forward, flexing his impressive physique. "We have the strength to do it. We're not just an anonymous group behind a screen; we're real people who have experienced the side effects of Vax-23 firsthand. We're here to expose the lies and protect our communities."

The live feed continued and they showcased their powers. Mark conjured a shimmering energy shield, Lydia demonstrated telekinesis by levitating objects around the room, and Elena created an illusion of shifting shadows that captivated viewers. Sylvia zipped around the bunker, leaving a trail of sparks in her wake, while Alex lifted heavy objects effortlessly, exhibiting his immense strength.

"Together, we are the Vanguard Coalition," Mark concluded, his voice resonating with authority. "We will not back down. We are committed to unveiling the truth and ensuring that you, the public, are informed and protected. Stand with us, let's fight for what's right."

As the live feed ended, the group stood together, a palpable sense of purpose enveloping them. They had crossed a threshold, unveiling their identities as superheroes while attempting to protect their personal lives.

They were no longer just a coalition; they had become symbols of hope and resistance.

In the hours following their broadcast, social media exploded with activity. Hashtags like #VanguardCoalition, #Vax23Truth, and #HeroesAmongUs trended on multiple platforms. Thousands of viewers had tuned in to watch the live feed, and the comments section was a battleground of opinions.

On Twitter, one user tweeted, "I've always been skeptical about the V-23 vaccine. Seeing the Vanguard Coalition step forward like this gives me hope! #VanguardCoalition"

Another comment read, "These guys are obviously just trying to distract us from the truth. The vaccine is safe! #StopTheMisinformation"

As the night wore on, a new narrative began to emerge. People started sharing their own experiences with Vax-23, some echoing the coalition's concerns about adverse effects while others shared stories of their loved ones who had faced complications. Videos began to surface of individuals discussing their personal battles with vaccine-related issues.

A viral TikTok video featured a young woman expressing her gratitude to the coalition: "I had no idea what was happening to me after I got the vaccine. I thought it was just me! Hearing these heroes say it's okay to question what we've been told – it's empowering! Thank you, Vanguard Coalition!"

Still, alongside the support came a barrage of attacks. Politicians and media pundits slammed the coalition, branding them as "dangerous conspiracy theorists" and "fearmongers." An article titled "Vanguard Coalition: Heroes or Hoaxes?" flooded news sites, questioning the validity of their claims and the integrity of their identities.

In the bunker, the coalition members watched the responses unfold, their emotions a whirlwind of anxiety and determination.

"We knew it wouldn't be easy, but look at how many people are rallying around us," Lydia said, her voice tinged with hope.

"Yeah, but the backlash is intense," Alex replied, frowning as he scrolled through a news article attacking their integrity. "They're framing us as a threat to public health."

Mark paced the room, contemplating their next steps. "We have to stay ahead of this; we need to continue providing credible information and supporting those who have suffered because of Vax-23."

Sylvia nodded enthusiastically. "Let's organize a follow-up live event! We can invite some of the people who shared their stories with us to join. It'll help humanize the issue."

Elena chimed in, her brow furrowed with thought. "We can show evidence of the side effects and how they correlate with the vaccine. If we present it well, we can build a stronger case."

The group brainstormed ideas for their next live event, determined to bolster their message and support their growing community. They worked late into the night, planning every detail, hoping to create a space where others could share their experiences and amplify their voices.

Days later, the Vanguard Coalition set up for another live event, this time in a large, public space that allowed for more interaction. They invited individuals who had experienced adverse reactions to Vax-23, hoping to create an honest conversation about the realities of their experiences.

As the camera began to roll, Mark addressed the audience as Quantum Blaze. "Welcome back, everyone. We are the Vanguard Coalition, and today we're here to continue our conversation about Vax-23 and the impact it's had on so many lives."

MindWave stood beside him, her demeanor serious. "We know that many of you are scared and confused. You're not alone. Today, we want to hear your stories and provide a platform for those affected by the vaccine."

One by one, the guests shared their experiences, recounting their journeys with honesty and vulnerability. Viewers tuned in, captivated by the raw emotion and truthfulness of each story. The comments flooded in, with many expressing solidarity and support, while others began to question their own beliefs about the vaccine.

The event progressed and Mark felt a swell of hope. They were creating a space for truth to emerge, countering the narrative that had been imposed on them. The coalition had become a movement for accountability and transparency. In the days that followed, their momentum continued to build, and the public's response grew more passionate. They had ignited a flame of inquiry and resilience that could no longer be extinguished.

Meanwhile, in the Oval Office, President Walker sat with his advisors, reviewing the live event. The tension in the room was perceptible. "This coalition is becoming a real threat," he said, his fingers steepled beneath his chin. "They've turned the narrative against us, and they're gaining public support."

Angela glanced at the screen, where comments were still pouring in from thousands of viewers. "We are still working to identify their members and disrupt their operations. This won't go on unchecked. We have searched the homes of agents we suspect may be leaking information, but nothing was discovered. We are still unsure of how they obtained such information."

"Every hour they gain traction makes it harder for us to control the message," Walker said, frustration evident in his voice. "I want all resources dedicated to countering this narrative. We need to discredit them before it spirals further out of control..."

17

The Showdown

T he night was thick with tension as the Vanguard
Coalition prepared for their next public gathering. Unbeknownst to them, a government task force
had devised a plan to undermine their momentum. In
a dimly lit conference room in the heart of the White
House, President Walker's advisors plotted their trap.

"Let's draw them out," Angela proposed, her voice
steady but her eyes gleaming with determination. "We
can stage a 'spontaneous' public debate on Vax-23,
promising the chance for the coalition to present their
case. We'll have our agents ready to move in as soon as
they show up."

President Walker nodded, a thin smile creeping
across his face. "Let's make them think they have the
upper hand. We'll cut their voices off before they can
gather any more support."

At the Vanguard Coalition's headquarters, Mark and
Lydia had been briefing the team about the potential
event. "This could be a perfect opportunity for us,"

Lydia said, looking at her fellow heroes. "Still, we need to be cautious. The government won't sit idly by."

Quantum Blaze, clad in radiant blue and gold, nodded. "I can create a force field to protect us while we speak. We'll need to keep the audience safe too." His ability to manipulate quantum energy would be crucial to protecting civilians and the team if things turned hostile.

"MindWave," Elena said, turning to their telepathic ally, "you need to be ready to sense any hostile intentions from the crowd. If anything feels off, we need to get out of there."

"I'll keep everyone calm," Lydia replied, her face displaying her ever-common brow furrowed in concentration. "I'll also prepare for any mental interference from the government."

Steelheart cracked his knuckles, his impenetrable skin glistening under the fluorescent lights. "If it comes down to a fight, I'll make sure we hold our ground."

Twilight Guardian, shrouded in shadows, smirked. "I'll provide cover. Let's make sure they don't see what's coming."

ChronoSpectra paced, her energy electric. "If we need to move fast, I'll get us out of any tight spots."

With their plan in place, they set out for the event, unaware of the trap that lay waiting.

As the night unfolded, a large crowd gathered in front of a makeshift stage in a community center. The air buzzed with excitement and anxiety. The Vanguard Coalition team took their places, ready to address the audience.

"Thank you all for coming," Quantum Blaze began, his voice strong. "We're here to discuss your experiences with Vax-23. This is your platform." As he turned, he made eye contact with Dr. Hayes, the head of the research team that he had spoken with when his symptoms first appeared. She had warned him to keep his abilities hidden – would she recognize him and expose his true identity? His heart raced at the thought, but he stayed calm and continued to speak. There were clearly others who experienced superhuman side effects, maybe she wouldn't be able to recognize it was him...

While they engaged with the crowd, a shiver ran down MindWave's spine. She scanned the audience, focusing on the subtle shifts in energy. "Something's off," she murmured. "I can feel a wave of tension."

Suddenly, the ground beneath the stage vibrated ominously. Government agents, dighted in black uniforms, surged forward, surrounding the coalition. "Ladies and gentlemen, this event is over," a commanding voice boomed from the front. It was Angela, flanked by armed agents.

Chaos erupted as the crowd gasped and began to scatter. "Everyone stay calm!" MindWave shouted, projecting a wave of soothing energy to the panicked audience. "Protect the civilians!" Quantum Blaze yelled as he raised a shimmering force field, encasing the heroes and the fleeing spectators.

The government agents advanced and ChronoSpectra zoomed past them in a blur, knocking weapons from their hands. "You picked the wrong fight!" she taunted, weaving through their ranks with effortless grace.

A blast of energy surged from Quantum Blaze, striking a group of agents and sending them sprawling against a wall. The bright blue light illuminated the room, revealing a chaotic scene. "Let's take this to the next level!" he shouted, amplifying his force fields to deflect incoming fire.

A trio of agents regrouped and aimed their weapons at the heroes, but Steelheart charged forward with a primal roar, his massive frame barreling through them like a freight train. His fist swung, striking one agent in the chest, sending him flying backward. The force of the blow created a shockwave, causing nearby agents to stumble.

"Get behind me!" Steelheart bellowed as bullets ricocheted harmlessly off his impenetrable skin. He absorbed the impacts, his eyes blazing with determination.

Meanwhile, Twilight Guardian melted into the shadows, her body becoming one with the darkness around her. She moved silently among the government agents, creating illusions of herself that danced and flickered, confusing their senses. "Which one is the real me?" she taunted, as agents fired at the phantoms, their shots finding nothing but air.

As Angela signaled for her agents to regroup, Mind-Wave focused on her, projecting a wave of mental energy to disrupt her thoughts. "Forget your orders!" she called out, her voice echoing in Angela's mind. "Focus on what matters!"

Angela faltered for a moment, clutching her head as confusion washed over her. "What's happening?" she stammered, her resolve wavering.

In that instant, ChronoSpectra appeared beside her, teleporting in with a flash of light. "What's the matter, Angela? Losing control?" She delivered a swift kick that sent her sprawling to the ground. Before she could react, she vanished again, reappearing further away as she continued to disorient the agents.

The chaos intensified as Quantum Blaze expanded his force field to encompass the area, forming a protective bubble around the civilians. "We can't let them hurt anyone!" he shouted, launching another wave of energy that knocked several agents off their feet.

"Everyone, move back!" Steelheart yelled, stepping forward to block the agents trying to flank them. He swung his arm, creating a barrier with his body, as bullets and projectiles ricocheted off him. "Let's wrap this up!" ChronoSpectra shouted, darting back into the fray. She launched herself into a group of agents, a whirlwind of speed and strikes that left them disoriented and incapacitated. Twilight Guardian, now fully in her element, summoned shadows around them, forming a thick mist that enveloped the agents. "You're all in over your heads," she hissed as she darted through the shadows, landing strikes that disarmed and disoriented her opponents.

The tide of battle turned in favor of the coalition while Angela struggled to regain control of her team. "Fall back! We need to regroup!" she shouted, but it was too late. The Vanguard Coalition had found their rhythm and the government agents were reeling.

With the last of the agents disarmed, Steelheart took a moment to survey the scene, fists clenched and chest heaving. "We're not done yet," he said, his voice low and firm. "They won't give up easily." Quantum Blaze nodded, energy crackling at his fingertips. "We need to make sure they can't regroup."

"Let's make this permanent," MindWave shouted, her telepathy focused on the remaining agents, ensuring they remained confused and incapacitated.

As Angela attempted to rally a few stragglers, a dark figure materialized behind her – Twilight Guardian emerged from the shadows with a triumphant grin. "Surprise!" she exclaimed, before incapacitating her with a well-placed blow.

With Angela down and her forces scattered, the heroes stood victorious, the crowd erupting in cheers and applause. Mark raised his fist in the air, a symbol of their triumph. "This is just the beginning!" he shouted, his voice carrying over the exhilarated crowd.

The cheers of the crowd echoed around them, ChronoSpectra took a deep breath and focused. "We need to get everyone to safety," she said, glancing at the panicked civilians still milling about. With a flash of speed, she created a series of portals, each shimmering with energy. "Step through; it's safe!" she urged, guiding families and individuals into the portals that would transport them to a secure city park a few blocks away.

Once the last citizen stepped through, Quantum Blaze nodded, reinforcing the protective barrier around the area. With a wave of his hand, he conjured a final pulse of energy that illuminated the surroundings. "Let's move, team!" he called, and in unison, the Vanguard Coalition stepped into one of ChronoSpectra's portals.

In an instant, they were back at their secret base in Avondale, the familiar surroundings enveloping them in a comforting embrace. The lights flickered on, revealing their headquarters, a sanctuary amidst the chaos. Mark let out a sigh of relief, his heart racing from the adrenaline of the night. "We did it," he said, looking around at his team. They had fought bravely, and together they had not only protected the innocent but also solidified their mission to hold those in power accountable. The Vanguard Coalition had proven that truth and accountability would prevail against any force seeking to silence them. As they settled in, the heroes knew their work was far from over, but tonight, they had won a crucial battle.

18

A Delicate Matter

The glow of the Phoenix skyline stretched out in front of Mark as he sat outside at his place, the late afternoon sun reflecting off the stretched-out desert before him. His heart raced – not from the thrill of the showdown, but from an email that had shattered his sense of security.

Subject: A Delicate Matter

Dear Mark,

I know it is you as head of the Vanguard Coalition. We need to meet. I have something vital to share.

— Elara

Mark rubbed his temples, a knot of anxiety tightening in his gut. The potential fallout of this revelation could be catastrophic, not just for him but for the entire coalition. Would she expose them? Headlines splashed across every news outlet about the showdown that had just happened, exposure of their true identities could devastate their mission. Even worse, it would put everyone in danger. He glanced around, half-expecting a shadowy figure to emerge from the desert's depths, ready to betray him.

After a moment of silent deliberation, he pulled out his phone and typed a response.

Subject: Re: A Delicate Matter
Dr. Hayes,
I'm listening. Where and when?
— Mark

Elara's reply was swift, guiding him to a small coffee shop near the Arizona State University campus. It was a vibrant spot, alive with students and adorned with eclectic art, the rich aroma of roasted beans mingling with the sound of laughter. Mark arrived early, slipping into a booth in the back, his mind swirling with worst-case scenarios.

When she walked in, Mark barely recognized her. Dr. Hayes had always been more at home in lab coats than street clothes. Today, however, she radiated confidence, her hair pulled back adorning her casual outfit, her frame silhouetted by the late afternoon sun.

"Mark," she greeted, her tone earnest. "Thank you for coming."

He nodded, gesturing for her to sit as he looked around expecting agents to swarm him again. "You said you had something important to share. What's going on?"

Elara leaned in, her voice low. "I assisted in the creation of the vaccine. I was part of a project that experimented with the gene-editing technology that led to it. What you're capable of... it's my fault."

Mark's brows furrowed, anger and confusion churning within him. "Fault? I think that's an understatement. Do you know how life-changing this has been? Do you even have any idea how many have been affected?"

She let out a sigh as she frowned. "No, but I do see that it came with consequences... Mark, I've developed abilities of my own – abilities that stem from my work in genetics. I can manipulate genetic sequences in real-time, enhance myself and others temporarily, and even counteract certain genetic anomalies."

His skepticism bubbled up. "Did you do this on purpose?!"

"No! Of course not!" Tears swelled in her eyes. "I didn't know it would go this far, I was truly trying to respond to the virus. I didn't know the companies and

government I worked for were so corrupt. It was igno-
rant of me... but I want to fix it. I want to join Vanguard."

Mark was taken aback, this was not what he expected.
He was prepared for her to expose him, not herself – and
definitely not prepared for her to join Vanguard. "You
think that's enough to join the Vanguard Coalition? You
could just as easily be a plant for the government." His
angry response was fueled by the unease he felt at her
presence.

"I understand your hesitance," she said, her eyes
steady. "Truly, I want to help. I see what you are trying
to do and what the coalition stands for – I want to fight
alongside you. I will spend the rest of my life attempting
to right this wrong and ensure people are not experimented on again."

Mark studied her, weighing her words carefully. Her
conviction felt real, but doubt gnawed at him.

"Here," she said breaking the silence as she pushed
a folder across the table to him. "Invoices from Biocure, Helix, and MedovaCorp. showing the payouts giv-
en to President Walker and other politicians to endorse
Vax-23 and its quick rollout."

Mark's eyes widened as he scanned each page. With
the staggering amounts given, he couldn't believe what
he was holding. He looked up at Elara, astonished she

would give him this information. "Alright. I'll bring you to the group. If they don't trust you..."

"Then I'll understand," she interjected, her voice resolute. "I'm willing to earn that trust."

Later, in the secret underground lair of the Vanguard Coalition, the atmosphere was electric with tension. Mark paced before his team, each adorned in their superhero personas, their identities cloaked behind masks.

"Are you sure about this, Mark?" Lydia, asked, her tone skeptical. "I know it's a risk," he replied, his voice steady. "She has provided powerful information in regard to payouts – and she claims she has powers that could enhance our efforts."

Elena narrowed her eyes. "She could be a double agent. This is not something we take lightly."

"Let's hear her out," Mark insisted. "If she's genuine, she might be key to what we're trying to achieve."

The coalition members exchanged glances, uncertainty lingering in the air. Finally, Elara entered, blindfolded and escorted by Alex, her demeanor composed yet earnest.

"Thank you for allowing me to speak," she began, scanning the group with intent after her blindfold was removed. "I know you don't trust me, but I assure you, I want to help you protect the very people who are at risk because of the experiments I initiated."

Alex, dressed as Steelheart, crossed his arms, skepticism etched on his face. "How do we know you're not here to sabotage us?"

Elara's gaze held steady. "I can show you. My powers aren't just about manipulation; I can also reverse certain genetic changes. If any of you have been affected by harmful alterations from your powers, I can assist."

A murmur rippled through the group, their expressions shifting from suspicion to intrigue. Sylvia, as ChronoSpectra, stepped forward. "Prove it. Show us what you can do."

Elara nodded, the moment settling over them like a palpable charge. She focused her energy, raising her hand. A faint glow enveloped her, illuminating the room with a warm light. Suddenly, a strand of her hair shimmered, elongating and changing colors, morphing through vibrant shades before settling back into its original form.

"That's... incredible," Lydia admitted, her skepticism softening just a bit.

"Impressive trick," Elena said, crossing her arms tighter, though her posture relaxed slightly. "What if it's just that, a party trick? We need more than show-manship."

Elara took a breath, sensing their reluctance. "I've developed protocols for controlling my abilities, ensuring they won't spiral out of control. I want to contribute to your mission, to protect innocent lives. I've seen the ramifications of our... my work firsthand. I want to rectify it."

Mark felt the weight of his team's gazes upon him. He stepped forward, determination in his stance. "I believe she can be an asset, but I understand your reluctance. Let's keep her on a trial basis. She'll need to prove her intentions with every action."

The room fell silent, uncertainty hanging thick in the air. Elara nodded slowly, absorbing the gravity of the decision. "I'm ready to earn your trust. Just give me a chance."

"I suppose we can let her stay," Lydia said hesitantly. "One wrong move..."

"I understand," Elara replied, her voice steady, though she could feel the weight of their skepticism. "I won't betray your trust."

With a collective breath, the coalition members exchanged wary glances. Though they were still reluctant, the decision was made. "Welcome to the Vanguard

Coalition, Dr. Hayes," Mark said, a hint of a smile breaking through the tension.

The air in the room shifted. Together, they would navigate the complexities of trust, power, and the hidden shadows of their pasts. A fragile truce forged in uncertainty with the path ahead unclear.

19
Elara

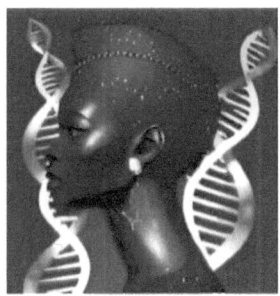

Genetica

D r. Elara Hayes had always felt the weight of the world pressing down on her, but it wasn't until her father's words echoed in her mind that she truly understood her purpose. "You have the power to change lives, Elara. Don't ever forget..."

Born in a small town in Idaho, Elara grew up in a modest home filled with the scent of pine and the crisp mountain air. Her father, Dr. Thomas Hayes, was a dedicated microbiologist whose passion for science was only matched by his unwavering love for his daughter. Elara's childhood was framed by long walks through the woods, where Thomas would explain the wonders of nature, teaching her to appreciate the intricate details of life. He often used these moments to inspire her curiosity, weaving lessons on biology into stories about the world around them.

Thomas was a single parent, having lost his wife when Elara was just a toddler. He often joked that he had been "stuck with a brilliant scientist in the making." Their home was filled with books on genetics and biology, models of DNA structures, and posters of the human genome. This nurturing environment ignited Elara's fascination with the possibilities of genetic science from a young age.

As Elara progressed through school, she excelled academically but struggled socially. While her peers were busy playing sports or gossiping, she was buried in her textbooks, poring over the latest discoveries in genetic research. The teasing from classmates for being "the science nerd" stung, but her father's encouragement always pulled her through. "You're destined for greatness," he'd tell her. "Never let others dim your light."

When it came time for college, Elara earned a scholarship to a prestigious university, where she immersed herself in the study of biology. Her determination drove her to spend long hours in the lab, often losing track of time as she meticulously conducted experiments. It was there that she first learned of the burgeoning field of genetic modification. Inspired, she vowed to harness this power for good, envisioning a future where genetic diseases could be eradicated and human potential enhanced.

Elara graduated with honors and continued her education, pursuing a doctorate in genetics. During her time in graduate school, she became a leading voice in the field, focusing on gene-editing technologies like CRISPR. Her work caught the attention of influential researchers and she quickly rose through the ranks, often participating in high-stakes discussions about the ethical implications of genetic manipulation.

Years later, while working at a renowned biotechnology firm, she was presented with an opportunity that would change everything. The company had been tasked with developing a vaccine for a novel virus that had begun to spread globally, V-23. As a key member of the research team, Elara's expertise in gene-editing technologies proved invaluable. She pushed the boundaries of science, exploring how to adapt and enhance the human immune system.

However, the process was fraught with ethical dilemmas. During late-night discussions with her colleagues, Elara voiced her concerns about the long-term consequences of their modifications. "We're playing with fire," she warned. "These changes could have unintended side effects. We need to ensure we're not creating more problems than we're solving."

Her passion shone through, but the pressure to deliver results was immense. Ultimately, her innovative approach yielded Vax-23, but it came with unexpected consequences: many who received it experienced adverse reactions – some began to manifest superhuman abilities. Even worse, they did not understand why some would have severe reactions, such as death, or why a small amount became superhuman; nor did they know exactly how many were superhuman.

As the chaos unfolded, Elara felt a deep sense of responsibility. She had inadvertently unleashed an array of side effects, and potential threats. Unable to shake off the weight of her involvement, she began to contemplate her role in this new world. In an attempt to understand the vaccine, she volunteered for a clinical trial. She was confident, in the beginning, that the vaccine would eliminate the virus with minor side effects. She quickly learned she was wrong when she began to experience her own superhuman abilities. Her skills in genetics had opened doors, but they also left her feeling vulnerable.

As far as she could tell, she was the only one who experienced these symptoms in this particular trial. Her abilities allowed her to manipulate genetic sequences and enhance the powers of others. Following the trial's overall success involving its impact on the virus, a meeting was held involving the companies' Board of Directors. Dr. Hayes attempted to raise concerns over adverse effects, but before she could even expose herself, she was shut down by higher-ups who reminded her they owned her research and could use it how they wished, and that the overall profit of the company determined that the vaccine must move forward towards mass distribution – no matter her concerns.

Elara quickly realized she had to keep her identity secret, especially from government agencies that might want to exploit her work. That's when she decided to find a way to utilize her knowledge and powers for good. With her background in genetics, she became Genetica.

Balancing her dual life was no easy task. By day, she was a respected geneticist; by night, she pursued avenues that may allow her to right her wrong. That's when she came across information advertising the debate the government was hosting with a new coalition called "Vanguard." Elara realized this might be the avenue she was seeking. As Genetica, she could use her abilities for good by assisting fellow heroes, using her powers to enhance their abilities, heal the genetic ailments of heroes and civilians, and thwart those who would misuse scientific advancements.

Now, as she sat in her hotel room in Phoenix after meeting with Mark and the other members of the
coalition, Elara stared at the bustling city below, the
amber street lights glowing against the backdrop of the
dusky sky. The plush surroundings of the hotel felt a
world away from the struggles of her past. Yet, a storm
brewed within her, fueled by the weight of her choices.
She would meet with Mark and the Vanguard Coalition
again to discuss their next plan, and a sense of anticipation mixed with trepidation filled the air.

Later that evening, in the dimly lit underground lair
of the Vanguard Coalition, Elara stepped into a space
brimming with energy. This time, she was there as a
member of the group – finally, she found a place where
she could attempt to right this wrong. The team was
gathered, their uniforms hiding their identities as a
testament to their distrust in Elara. Mark stood at the
center, his presence commanding as he introduced her,
"Everyone, I present to you Dr. Elara Hayes, Genetica."

MindWave eyed her warily. Twilight Guardian
crossed her arms. "We're still not entirely convinced
you're on our side," she said.

"I understand," Elara replied, her voice steady. "...the corruption within the government is deeper than you know. I want to expose it, but I need your help. Together, we can make them tell the truth."

"What do you propose?" Steelheart asked, leaning forward, intrigue mixing with skepticism.

Elara took a breath, her resolve firming. "We need to take a bold approach. Instead of just gathering evidence, we should infiltrate President Walker's vacation house. We confront him directly, make it clear that he must expose the corruption or face serious consequences."

Quantum Blaze raised an eyebrow, the gravity of her words hanging in the air. "You're suggesting we confront the President in-person?"

"Exactly," Elara said, her eyes blazing with determination. "If we can reach him despite his security detail, we can make him understand the urgency of the situation. We'll lay out the evidence we have and make it clear that if he doesn't act, we will hold him directly accountable."

The room fell silent as the implications of her plan settled in. MindWave's skepticism deepened. "What if he refuses to listen?"

"Then we'll have to make it clear that we're a force to be reckoned with," Elara replied, her voice gaining strength. "He needs to understand that we're not just heroes; we're willing to take action against those who exploit their power. We can scare him into making a choice: change his ways or face the consequences. The people deserve to know the truth."

ChronoSpectra nodded slowly, her initial wariness giving way to intrigue. "This could work, but we'll need a solid plan. What's our exit strategy? The security around him will be tight."

"We'll go in stealthily," Elara explained. "I can use my genetic manipulation to help us blend in. With a little finesse, I can alter our appearances enough to bypass some of the initial security checks. Once we're inside, we'll present our case directly. If he still refuses, we'll use our abilities to make it clear we mean business. We'll ensure he knows we're not just another group of vigilantes. We are the Vanguard Coalition and we're here to enforce justice."

"Timing is everything," Quantum Blaze interjected, pacing slightly. "We need to know when he's most vulnerable. His vacation house will likely be full of agents, but if we can catch him when he's having a private moment – maybe during a morning run or while he's out on the patio – we'll have our chance."

Elara nodded, adrenaline coursing through her veins. "We can gather intel on his schedule. Once we have a window, we move in. I'll use my abilities to keep us hidden while we get to him. This has to be quick and decisive. We'll confront him with everything we have – proof of the corruption, the manipulation of the V-23 project, and the public's need for accountability."

The atmosphere in the room shifted as her words ignited a flicker of hope. Each member of the coalition could see the potential in this audacious plan – a chance to hold the highest office accountable and reclaim the narrative. The room buzzed with discussions, ideas flying back and forth. Though the coalition remained somewhat reluctant, a shared vision began to form, creating a discernible energy in the air.

20

The Brink of Revelation

The moon sat high in the night sky, casting silvery light over the secluded coastal estate of President Walker. Surrounded by towering pines and the rhythmic sound of the waves, the vacation house was a deceptive facade of tranquility. Inside, however, it was anything but peaceful.

In the dark, shadows slinked along the walls, moving with purpose. Twilight Guardian stepped forward, her form melding with the darkness like ink spreading across parchment. "All clear," she whispered, her voice a ghostly murmur, blending seamlessly with the sounds of the ocean.

"Time to make our entrance," Quantum Blaze replied, his eyes glowing faintly with quantum energy as he prepared to project a force field. The air hummed with anticipation as the team gathered around him, ready for the confrontation that lay ahead.

"Are we really going through with this plan?" ChronoSpectra questioned, her brow furrowed with concern. She shifted her weight from one foot to the other, her heart racing. "Confronting the President is one thing, but threatening him..."

"It's not just a threat," Steelheart interjected, his voice steady, resonating with the confidence of a man who had faced worse odds. "It's a promise. The American people deserve the truth, especially when lives hang in the balance. Vax-23 is just the tip of the iceberg."

"Let's focus," chimed in MindWave, her tone brisk and efficient, her energy practically vibrating with urgency. "We need to be in and out before anyone knows we're here. The last thing we want is a media circus."

Genetica altered their appearance to blend in as Secret Service agents. With a nod, Quantum Blaze launched his force field, enveloping the group in a shimmering bubble that refracted the dim light of the room as they slipped through the French doors leading to the living room. Inside, the air was thick with the scent of aged wood and saltwater, the soft sounds of jazz playing from a vintage record player juxtaposing the tension that filled the air.

As the force field dissipated, the heroes stood poised, ready for anything. President Walker lounged on a leather sofa, a drink in hand, but his eyes widened in disbelief as he took in the sight of the Vanguard Coalition, a mix of surprise and indignation crossing his features.

"Who—how did you get in here?" he stammered, glancing toward the window as if considering escape.

"Relax, Mr. President," Twilight Guardian said, her voice smooth and calm, her presence a dark whisper in the dim light. "We're here for a friendly chat. We want to discuss Vax-23." Seeing they were alone, Genetica revealed their appearance as superheroes.

The President's brow furrowed, a flicker of fear darting through his eyes as he saw them shift into their uniforms. "I don't know what you're talking about," he stammered.

"Liar," MindWave said, stepping closer, her empathy weaving a thread between them. As she reached into his mind, she sifted through his memories and fears, feeling the hot pulse of anxiety that lay just beneath his bravado. "You know exactly what we're talking about. The experiments, the cover-ups, and the lives put at risk for corporate gain. It all ends tonight."

"Do you think you can just barge in here and intimidate me?" Walker shot back, his voice rising defensively. "I won't be threatened by a bunch of – "

"Superheroes?" Quantum Blaze cut in, energy crackling at his fingertips as he took a step forward, a force field shimmering at his side. "That's exactly what we are, and we're here to ensure that you expose the corruption that has plagued this government for too long. Don't believe me? Look at what we can leak next," he warned as he tossed the folder containing the payout information to Walker and others from Biocure, Helix, and MedovaCorp.

Walker grabbed the file, a shocked look appeared on his face as he read. "You're talking about the very foundations of power," Walker retorted, his face hardening into a mask of defiance. "Do you know what would happen if I went public with this? It would shatter everything!"

"Good," Steelheart said, his tone unwavering as he leaned closer, his massive frame looming like a sentinel. "What you're protecting now is poison. You have a choice: stand with the people or continue to hide behind your political games. If you don't act, we will."

Genetica added, "You think you can keep this quiet? The truth will come out one way or another, and we'll make sure the right people are held accountable. Your inaction is complicity."

"Your threats mean nothing to me," Walker said, though his voice wavered slightly, the fear creeping in despite his grandiosity. "I'm not afraid of you."

"Then you haven't been paying attention," Twilight Guardian replied, her eyes glinting with shadows, a smirk dancing on her lips. "We can do more than threaten. We'll expose every hidden deal, every corrupt figure backing you, and we'll take action."

MindWave stepped even closer, her presence a soothing balm amidst the tension. "We're not your enemies, Mr. President. We don't want violence, but if you force our hand, we won't hesitate to show the world the truth. The people deserve to know what you've done, and we will not allow you to bury it any longer."

The room fell silent, the weight of the moment settling over them like a heavy fog. Walker's bravado cracked, revealing uncertainty beneath. He glanced at the six figures surrounding him, each a beacon of power and resolve, their eyes burning with righteous determination.

"You really believe you can just overthrow the government?" he asked, doubt creeping into his tone, the hint of a tremor beneath the surface.

"Do you really believe you could stop us?" Steelheart replied with his voice low, almost a growl. "If it comes to that, we will. We believe in a better future – one that doesn't depend on lies and deceit. It doesn't have to come from violence. You still have the chance to do the right thing."

Walker swallowed hard, weighing the options laid before him. The pressure built, thick and suffocating, as the heroes watched him, unwavering. The soft sound of waves crashing against the shore punctuated the silence, a reminder of the world outside this moment.

"You have until dusk tomorrow," Quantum Blaze stated, stepping closer, his energy flickering like a flame. "By then, we'll be watching to see if you stand with us or against us."

As they turned to leave, the soft click of the door handle echoed through the quiet room. Just then, the sound of hurried footsteps approached from the hallway. Steelheart's instincts kicked in. "We need to move. Now!"

"Wait!" MindWave exclaimed, her eyes darting toward the source of the noise. "We can't let them see us."

Genetica quickly shifted their appearance in an attempt to disguise the group. Before they could react, the door swung open, and two Secret Service men burst in, their faces set in grim determination, weapons drawn. "Get your hands up! Now!" One of them barked, scanning the room for threats.

Time slowed as the Vanguard Coalition reacted. Quantum Blaze flicked his wrist, conjuring a shimmering barrier between the heroes and the guards, while Twilight Guardian melted back into the shadows, ready to strike from the darkness.

"Fire!" Walker shouted, rising from the sofa, hands raised in a fretted gesture. "They're here to hurt me!"

"Secure the area!" one guard shouted, his eyes darting between the President and the intruders, confusion evident on his face.

MindWave took a step forward, her demeanor calm and authoritative. "We're here to help, but if you don't stand down, this can escalate quickly."

Steelheart crossed his arms, his physique imposing. "We don't want a fight, but we won't hesitate to defend ourselves."

"They're the enemy!" Walker insisted, stepping forward, his voice steadying as he looked at the guards. "They've come to cause me harm. Shoot!"

The guards hesitated, glancing at each other, uncertainty creeping into their stance. "What do you mean? What's going on?" One of them finally asked, lowering his weapon slightly. MindWave had entered their minds, causing hesitation and confusion.

Quantum Blaze seized the moment, lowering his force field just enough to show he meant no harm. "We're exposing corruption, and if President Walker doesn't do the right thing, we will take matters into our own hands."

Walker stepped forward, his authority flickering but still present. "Don't listen to them. They're lying. I am the President! I give the commands!"

Slowly, the tension in the room began to ease as the guards, still wary, lowered their weapons but kept them at the ready. The President's conviction did not seem to sway them, at least for the moment.

"Your time is running out, Walker," Quantum Blaze warned, stepping back, ready to teleport if necessary. "We'll be watching closely. Remember, dusk tomorrow."

With that, they slipped back into the shadows, the guards still on edge and unsure of how to proceed. The confrontation had escalated, and now the stakes were higher than ever.

As the Vanguard Coalition vanished into the night, Walker stood at the center of the room, flanked by security, contemplating the monumental decision ahead. Would he choose the path of truth, or continue down the dark road paved by corruption? Outside, the world awaited, oblivious to the storm that was about to break.

21

Shadows of Authority

The walls of the Oval Office felt oppressive today as if they were closing in on President Walker. He stood behind the massive mahogany desk, the golden presidential seal gleaming under the soft light, his mind a whirlwind of last night's events.

The warning had come as a shock when the six members of the Vanguard Coalition stormed into his vacation house, their presence a stark contrast to the polished decorum of the space. Walker had felt a surge of indignation. The audacity of these so-called heroes! How dare they threaten him in his own home!

Now, standing in the daylight, he reflected on their faces – so determined, so sure of their moral high ground. Still, that didn't matter. He had a country to run, and they were a liability.

"Mr. President?" Angela, his Chief of Staff, broke into his reverie, her brow knitted with concern. She stepped into the room, the echoes of last night still hanging in the air. "I am glad you've returned safely. We need to discuss the Vanguard's warning."

"They think they can intimidate us," he replied, pacing to the window. He could see the Washington skyline, a glittering reminder of power and authority. "We won't give in. We need to take back control."

"By what means?" Angela asked, crossing her arms. "We can't simply dismiss them. This could lead to a public outcry. Their tactics and exposure have led the public to believe they are good."

Walker turned, his blue eyes fierce with determination. "We need to disband the coalition. First, I'll sign an executive order requiring citizens to report any side effects from Vax-23 to the government. We need to create a narrative that puts us in charge of the discussion."

"...and then?" she prompted, knowing what he was hinting towards.

"Then we add the Vanguard members to the domestic terrorist list. This is about securing the nation, Angela. They are a threat, and if they want to play the hero, they'll face the consequences."

Angela hesitated, her instincts battling with the weight of their reality. "Sir, that could escalate the situation. We might incite violence. Requiring the public to regist—"

"Let them escalate," he interjected sharply. "If they want a fight, we'll show them what real power looks like. I want increased military presence throughout the cities – deploy National Guard units to patrol the streets, and I want special operations teams on standby."

"Are you sure about this?" she asked, voice steady but worried. "Requiring registered side effects and labeling the Vanguard as terrorists could galvanize their support."

"They're already organizing," he replied, clenching his jaw. "We can't wait. If they're plotting something, we need to be one step ahead."

In the days that followed, Walker's resolve turned into a frenzy of activity. The administration mobilized quickly. Press conferences were held with military officials standing behind him, creating an imposing presence. Walker's rhetoric was sharp, framing the Vanguard's warning as a cowardly assault on democracy. The new measures passed swiftly, the legislation aimed at requiring the public to register adverse reactions to Vax-23 becoming a rallying cry for his supporters – and angering those who oppose.

Still, President Walker could not shake the warning. He was now looking over his shoulder, he had ignored their demands to expose everything by dusk the next day. "I'll get ahead of them, they won't be able to do anything," he tried to reassure himself as he poured a drink in an attempt to relax.

With each announcement, Walker could see the shifting tides. The military's involvement was palpable – National Guard units patrolled the streets, their uniforms a stark reminder of the government's authority. Special operations teams were deployed covertly, ready to act against any perceived threat from the Vanguard. The government's reaction to the Vanguard Coalition's warning was a complex, diversified strategy designed to suppress and neutralize the threat posed by the heroes. Through a combination of public relations efforts, increased security measures, legal actions, military responses, and covert operations, the government aimed to dismantle the coalition and restore control over the narrative and power structures.

Nevertheless, tensions escalated alongside the public's outrage. Protests erupted across major cities with citizens gathering in droves to voice their discontent. Signs reading "Heroes, Not Terrorists!" and "Transparency Now!" flooded the streets. Social media buzzed with calls to action, including videos of Vanguard supporters rallying, which circulated like wildfire.

Public sentiment swung sharply against Walker. He could feel the backlash as the protests grew larger and more passionate. Every time he appeared on television, the chants of dissent echoed in his ears – "We won't be silenced!" and "Expose the truth!" The streets became a cry of ideals, with citizens demanding accountability and veracity.

The next evening, as he prepared for a televised address, Angela entered the room, her face pale. "Sir, there's been a development. We think we have located the Vanguard's headquarters."

Walker felt his heart race. "How?"

"They've been gathering testimonies from individuals who experienced adverse effects from Vax-23," she replied, urgency tinging her voice. "One of these individuals has come forward claiming they know where the hideout is located."

"Then we need to act," he said, pacing. "Increase surveillance on the location. I want eyes everywhere. We cannot let them gain any momentum."

In the heart of the D.C., the divide deepened. The news reported crowds gathering outside the White House, people chanting for justice, their voices melding into a cacophony that reverberated through the air. Signs waved, the messages clear and defiant, igniting a fire that Walker hadn't anticipated. As footage rolled on screens nationwide, it was impossible to ignore the momentum building against him.

He knew he had pushed too far, yet he couldn't back down now. The stakes were too high, and in this game of power, he would do whatever it took to maintain control, even if it meant drawing battle lines in the sand. As Quantum Blaze's voice echoed in his mind, Walker prepared for the takedown, ready to turn the tide once and for all.

22

Innocent Attack

The fluorescent lights buzzed ominously in the sterile briefing room, amplifying the tension that hung in the air. President Walker stood at the front, flanked by military brass. His voice cut through the murmurs.

"Ladies and gentlemen," he said, his tone unwavering, "the Vanguard represents a threat to our sovereignty. Their vigilante justice is no longer acceptable. We have credible intelligence that they are plotting a significant operation. Our response must be decisive."

An officer pressed a button and a detailed map flickered onto the screen. Images of the Vanguard's alleged lair, a dilapidated industrial complex on the city's edge, flashed across the room.

"Phase One involves a full-scale raid," the officer continued, pointing to various locations. "Teams Alpha, Bravo, and Charlie will provide support. We expect heavy resistance."

The murmurs quieted, replaced by a palpable determination. Walker locked eyes with each officer. "We take no chances. This is about restoring order."

As night enveloped the city, black SUVs crept through shadowy streets. Special Ops teams, clad in tactical gear, exited quietly. The lead commander adjusted his headset, focused and resolute.

"Team Alpha, breach the northwest entrance. Bravo and Charlie, provide perimeter support. Move quickly."

Under the cover of darkness, they navigated the complex's periphery. A strange sense of foreboding settled in the pit of their stomachs as they spotted what appeared to be dark figures in the distance – silhouettes moving with precision, engaging in what may be a training exercise.

"Targets confirmed," the commander whispered, adrenaline surging. "Engage."

The teams burst through the heavy steel doors, the sound echoing like a gunshot in the stillness. The air thickened with tension as they flooded into the halls, weapons drawn, eyes scanning for any sign of the Vanguard.

Inside, the atmosphere was disconcertingly quiet. Empty rooms and scattered equipment hinted at a once-thriving hub of activity, now deserted. The teams moved cautiously, every creak and whisper amplified in the silence.

"Where is everyone?" a soldier muttered, glancing around nervously.

"Keep moving," the commander snapped, anxiety creeping into his voice. "They must be hiding."

Suddenly, alarms blared, red lights flashing as if the very walls were warning them of their impending mistake. The soldiers rushed deeper into the building, fueled by a mix of urgency and confusion. They stumbled into a large room filled with old pieces of large equipment. It was empty.

"Command, this is Alpha. We're inside, but we've found no signs of the Vanguard. Confirm our intel," the commander radioed, dread lacing his words.

"Negative, Alpha. You're at the right location. They must be preparing for something," the voice on the other end responded, a hint of frustration seeping through.

With each passing moment, tension escalated. The teams kicked down door after door, finding only remnants of training. Confusion turned into panic when they reached a central area filled with old monitors.

"Where are they?" one soldier shouted, slamming his fist on a table in frustration. Suddenly, a crackling transmission disrupted their chaos.

"Attention! You are not authorized to be here! Evacu-ate immediately!" the voice yelled, echoing through the halls, but it was too late.

"Keep searching!" the commander yelled, his heart racing. The squad's movements became frantic as they pushed deeper into the complex.

A group of operators rushed toward the side wing, dread gnawing at their insides. Kicking down the door, they were met with a horrifying sight – dozens of people crammed into a community center in what looked to be a converted makeshift shelter, their eyes wide with terror.

Before they could process the chaos, a few civilians instinctively reacted to the armed soldiers. A young man charged forward while another began to fire his gun. Unsure of who they were or why they were in the shelter, the people attempted to defend themselves. The operators responded, firing back in a knee-jerk reaction. Gunfire echoed as people screamed and ran in all directions.

A father stepped forward, fear etched on his face, raising his hands. "Please, we're just trying to keep our families safe!" he pleaded, confusion spilling from his voice. A mother clutched her child tightly, tears streaming down her cheeks, crying out, "What do you want from us?" The soldiers, momentarily frozen by the sight of these terrified families, felt the weight of their mistake. In that instant, the line between hero and villain blurred, as the realization hit them – these were not their enemies. They were innocent victims caught in a nightmare.

An operator burst into the main hall, face pale and eyes wide. "Commander! We've got civilians trapped in a side wing!"

"What do you mean civilians?" the commander's voice trembled with disbelief, a sickening feeling pooling in his stomach. "We were supposed to raid the Vanguard!"

They rushed toward the side wing, dread gnawing at their insides. As they entered through the already kicked-in doors, they were met with a horrifying scene – dozens of innocent civilians running and screaming, others laying in pools of blood with family clutching their lifeless bodies.

"Get medics in here, now!" the commander barked, heart heavy with guilt.

As the operators worked to reassure the frightened families and offer medical aid, the press began to gather outside, their cameras rolling, capturing the unfolding chaos.

Meanwhile, at a hidden location far from the chaos, the Vanguard Coalition sat glued to their screens. A massive monitor displayed live news coverage of the raid. They exchanged anxious glances, their expressions a mix of disbelief and horror.

"Turn it up!" shouted Lydia, her eyes fixed on the broadcast.

The anchor's voice crackled through the speakers. "A shocking scene as military forces engage in an attempted operation against the Vanguard. However, it appears that the raid has targeted a civilian community center instead of the superhero coalition's lair."

"Are they serious?" Alex gripped the edge of the table, his knuckles white. "This is a disaster."

"Those people are innocent," whispered Elena, her voice trembling with empathy. "We have to intervene."

As the camera zoomed in on terrified people, alongside what appeared to be bodies wrapped in black plastic, emerging from the complex, the reality of the situation began to sink in. The world was witnessing the consequences of a botched operation. The anchor continued, "Reports indicate that the military may have misidentified the location of the Vanguard Coalition, leading to unintended casualties."

The Vanguard members exchanged glances, knowing they had to act. With their hearts heavy, they prepared to step into the fray, determined to protect those caught in the crossfire of a misguided mission.

"Seems President Walker didn't take our warning seriously," Mark said, his voice steady. "It's time to clean this up ourselves." The team rallied, their resolve solidified by the injustice unfolding live on television.

As they donned their gear and prepared to intervene, the nation watched – shocked, outraged, and desperate for answers. The truth was unfolding, but the real battle was just beginning.

23

The Rising

The sunset over the capital cast an amber glow that illuminated the National Mall, where countless citizens had once gathered for protests demanding transparency and justice. Behind the walls of the White House, however, darkness brewed, a stark contrast to the bright facade presented to the public. President Walker paced his office, tension gnawing at him as he recalled the unsettling reports flooding in – the unusual energy signatures, the sudden disappearances of prominent whistleblowers. It was clear: the Vanguard Coalition was on the move.

The past few months had been chaos, citizens complained about the government's corruption, including their involvement with Vax-23 and the poorly planned raid against the Vanguard that harmed innocent civilians. It was clear to the public now that the vaccine had wreaked havoc, causing genetic mutations and severe health issues for hundreds of thousands around the world, all in the name of "progress." Citizens were

suffering, but their cries for help were drowned out
by government propaganda still touting Vax-23 as a
miracle cure.

Inside a dilapidated warehouse several blocks away,
the Vanguard Coalition assembled, their faces resolute
with the weight of their mission. Quantum Blaze adjusted his wrist gauntlet, energy pulsating around him in
a soft blue hue. "We have tried to civilly resolve this –
the raid that killed innocent civilians is the end of the
negotiations. It's time to take action. We all know what's
at stake. This isn't just about overthrowing a corrupt
government; it's about saving lives."

MindWave, her eyes shimmering with psychic energy, nodded gravely. "The people are rightfully scared.
They know they were manipulated into believing the
government had their best interest at heart. They need
us to right these wrongs, to fight for their true best
interests."

Twilight Guardian, wrapped in a cloak of shadows,
smirked. "Let's give them a show they won't forget.
We'll use their fear against them."

Steelheart crossed his arms, his skin gleaming like
steel. "I think they've learned that the Vanguard isn't
just a name – if they haven't, they're about to for sure."

ChronoSpectra, her fingers twitching with impa-
tience, chimed in. "We need to be quick. The military

is already on high alert. I can teleport us in, but we'll need a distraction to keep their attention elsewhere."

Genetica, her hair glimmering like stars, stepped forward. "I'll enhance your abilities before we engage. We need to strike decisively. The people deserve to see the truth about the corruption in the government, including Vax-23 and the regime that was forced upon them."

With a collective nod, the Vanguard Coalition steeled themselves. Quantum Blaze raised his hand and a shimmering force field enveloped them. "Let's show them what we're made of..."

The infiltration began with a blinding flash as ChronoSpectra accelerated, teleporting them through the barriers of the White House, landing silently in the darkened corridors. The first floor was eerily quiet, the faint hum of electronics and distant murmurs of guards were the only sounds breaking the silence.

"MindWave, can you read their thoughts?" Quantum Blaze whispered, keeping his voice low.

"I'm trying," she replied, closing her eyes as her forehead creased in concentration. "There are six guards near the entrance. They're alert but terrified. They suspect something is amiss."

"Perfect," Twilight Guardian said, her voice a blend of excitement and menace. "Let them underestimate us. I'll weave illusions to disorient their defenses."

MindWave concentrated, and with a flick of her wrist, she projected a wave of confusion into the guards' minds. They stumbled, seeing phantoms attacking from the outside, darting left and right as if besieged by a ghostly army.

"Now!" Quantum Blaze commanded, propelling himself forward, his energy shield deflecting the guards' gunfire as the rest of the team followed. Steelheart charged into the fray, his impenetrable skin absorbing bullets, which ricocheted harmlessly away.

As the guards scattered, Twilight Guardian stepped into the shadows, becoming a wraith among them, taking them down silently one by one. A guard turned, confusion painted across his face as he encountered only darkness.

In the chaos, MindWave amplified her mental power, reinforcing the illusions Twilight Guardian cast, turning the empty hallways into a labyrinth of fear. The guards found themselves battling shadows, unable to distinguish reality from hallucination.

In the Oval Office, President Walker's voice echoed over the intercom. "This is a lockdown! All units, report to your posts!"

ChronoSpectra, moving like a blur, teleported past security protocols, reaching the doorway of the Oval Office. "We're almost there! We need to end this now."

Walker was prepared. With the flick of a switch, he activated the emergency defenses. Barriers, rising like steel flowers from the ground, blocked the entrance.

"Steelheart, break through!" Quantum Blaze shouted, channeling energy into his hands.

With a mighty roar, Steelheart charged at the barriers. His fists connected with a thunderous impact, sending tremors through the room. The steel crumpled as he powered through, shattering the obstacle.

Inside the office, Walker stood defiantly, flanked by armed guards, his face a mask of resolve. "You think you can overthrow the government? You're nothing but vigilantes!"

"Vigilantes?" MindWave replied, stepping forward with confidence. "We're the ones who stand for justice! You've manipulated and betrayed the people long enough with your lies. People are suffering, and we know it's not just a vaccine; it's a genetic experiment! After all, you created us!"

Before he could retort, Quantum Blaze unleashed a concentrated energy blast, sending guards sprawling. The room flickered with power as MindWave swiftly disarmed another guard using her telekinesis, sending his weapon flying.

Twilight Guardian moved in like a shadow, taking advantage of the confusion, her form indistinguishable from the darkness. She launched an illusion of a swarm of bats that filled the room, causing panic among the guards.

Steelheart, a mountain of muscle, advanced toward Walker, a determined glint in his eye. "It's over, Walker. Your time is finished."

With a sudden surge, Walker activated a hidden mechanism, releasing a cloud of gas that filled the room. The Coalition recoiled, but Genetica stepped forward, her aura glowing with vibrant energy.

"Not today!" she shouted, infusing her teammates with a burst of enhanced resilience, countering the effects of the gas. They regained their composure, determination renewed.

"Your lies end here!" Quantum Blaze shouted, channeling energy into his hands. With a swift motion, he created a force field to shield them from the gas, his power manifesting in a dazzling display of blue light.

Walker found himself cornered, surrounded by the Vanguard. He fumbled for a last resort weapon, a device that hummed ominously. "You don't know what you're doing! The world needs order!" He choked out the words as he inhaled the gas and looked around for help.

"The world needs hope," MindWave declared, stepping forward with a fierce gaze. "We are that hope. Your Vax-23 was never about protecting the public. It was a means to control and exploit. Everything the government has implemented for years has been a means to control and exploit."

With a swift motion, she reached out, planting a mental anchor that she and Quantum Blaze had created. It incapacitated Walker, leaving him in a stupor. As he fell to the floor, he dropped the mysterious device. The coalition stood victorious, a united front against a crumbling regime.

Outside, sirens blared, but the Vanguard Coalition had ignited a spark of rebellion within the hearts of the citizens. The echoes of their battle reverberated through the building. The truth about Vax-23 and the government's corruption had spread like wildfire. With the President and other government figures overthrown, those left in the White House scrambled to evacuate. The government was in shambles.

Quantum Blaze turned to his teammates, the remnants of energy still crackling at his fingertips. "It's not over. We've exposed this regime for what it is, not just for ourselves but for every life they've destroyed. Now, we must rebuild."

Genetica nodded, her eyes gleaming with resolve. "Together, we will heal the wounds they've inflicted. The Vanguard Coalition is just getting started."

As they prepared to step into the light of a new dawn, their mission was clear: finish dismantling the system that had betrayed its people, one step at a time.

24

A New Dawn

The dust settled in Washington, D.C. as the Vanguard Coalition emerged from the shadows of rebellion. In the months following their decisive confrontation with President Walker, the once-feared heroes became symbols of hope and renewal. News of their actions spread quickly, igniting a wave of change that swept across the nation.

The first order of business for the coalition was to dismantle the corrupt infrastructure that had allowed Vax-23 and other injustices to thrive. Genetica led initiatives to ensure the safe and ethical handling of biotechnology, while MindWave worked tirelessly to gather testimonies from victims of the vaccine and other government abuses. Citizens who had suffered in silence now found their voices, their stories echoed in town halls and public forums as the coalition championed transparency.

In the heart of D.C., the Vanguard Coalition set up headquarters in the very building that once housed the Oval Office. They transformed the space into a community center where citizens could gather, share their experiences, and discuss the future of their country. The walls, once adorned with portraits of former leaders, now displayed vibrant murals depicting hope, resilience, and unity.

Months passed and the transformation of the nation was palpable. News broadcasts highlighted the coalition's reforms, including the establishment of a new Department of Health and Integrity, which would oversee all medical practices and research. This department mandated transparency in all pharmaceutical developments, ensuring that citizens were never again subjected to dangerous experiments without their knowledge. It also launched a comprehensive investigation into Vax-23, leading to the identification of those responsible for the program's corruption.

The Vanguard Coalition also created the "Healing America" initiative, a series of town hall meetings across the country aimed at directly addressing public grievances. Steelheart, known for his strength but also his compassion, traveled to small towns and urban centers alike, listening to the concerns of citizens and reinforcing their rights. In each community, he encountered stories of loss – families torn apart by the side effects of Vax-23 – but he also found a determination to heal and rebuild.

In the suburbs, families gathered in living rooms, watching live streams of the Vanguard members as they discussed policy changes. Parents spoke of the importance of educating their children about humanities, science, and ethics, eager to prevent history from repeating itself. Quantum Blaze made it a point to attend schools, sharing his story of empowerment and inspiring students to stand up for their rights.

As the coalition took to the streets, they encountered enthusiastic crowds. People waved banners adorned with the Vanguard emblem, cheering them on. "We are the Vanguard!" echoed through city squares, a chorus of unity and resolve that rang across the nation.

With their legitimacy firmly established, the coalition turned its attention to accountability for the previous administration. President Walker and his key allies faced intense scrutiny, with evidence mounting against their misdeeds. Vanguard formed an independent committee to investigate the abuses of power and corruption that had defined Walker's tenure. Whistleblowers, emboldened by the coalition's support, came forward with damning testimonies about Vax-23 and other clandestine operations.

After a thorough investigation, the former president and several high-ranking officials were indicted on charges ranging from negligence to criminal conspiracy. Public outrage fueled the demand for justice, and the trial captured the nation's attention. In an unprecedented move, the coalition broadcast the proceedings live, ensuring that every American could witness the unfolding of justice.

The atmosphere in the courtroom was electric as the former president sat before a jury, flanked by his once-loyal aides now turned witnesses. MindWave and her fellow members attended each day, their presence a reminder of the power of accountability.

As the trial progressed, evidence of Walker's direct involvement in the Vax-23 cover-up was unveiled. Testimonies from victims and whistleblowers painted a horrifying picture of a government willing to sacrifice its citizens for profit and power. It was a turning point for many; those who had once feared the Vanguard Coalition began to see them as champions of justice.

In a dramatic climax, the jury found Walker guilty on multiple counts and he was sentenced to twenty years in prison. His accomplices, including several senators and government officials, faced similar fates, receiving sentences ranging from ten to fifteen years. Angela, upon testifying and producing evidence against Walker and others involved, received a lighter sentence.

Leonard Blake, the CEO of Biocure; Marisol Grant, head of MedovaCorp.; and Thomas Reddick, Helix's CFO were all charged for their crimes, including bribery, fraud, producing false statements, endangering public health, and violations of drug safety and regulatory laws. They all received fines and prison sentences and were forced to step down from their positions. Furthermore, Vanguard worked to revoke the liability waivers allowing them to be subject to civil suits from those harmed by unsafe vaccines. The country erupted in a mix of relief and celebration. People took to the streets to express their gratitude to the Vanguard Coalition.

The months that followed were a time of healing and rebuilding. The coalition introduced reforms aimed at empowering citizens, ensuring that their voices would shape the future of governance. They established a series of community councils, giving ordinary citizens a platform to engage with their leaders and participate in decision-making.

As part of the "Healing America" initiative, the Vanguard Coalition implemented educational programs that focused on ethics in science and governance. Schools across the nation adopted curricula that emphasized critical thinking, transparency, and the importance of civic engagement. Children learned not just about their rights, but how to be proactive citizens, cultivating a generation that understood the value of accountability.

In urban neighborhoods and rural communities alike, residents reported a renewed sense of trust in their government. The focus on community-led initiatives sparked hope and empowerment. Citizens felt they were not just passive observers but active participants in shaping their government. Local businesses began to thrive as the new government emphasized small business support, creating grants that revitalized struggling communities.

In a pivotal moment of unity, the coalition hosted a nationwide event, the "Unity Festival," to celebrate the progress made, and to recognize the resilience of the American people. Music filled the air, families gathered for food and games, and testimonials were shared from citizens whose lives had been transformed.

MindWave stood on stage, her heart swelling with pride as she addressed the crowd. "This is just the beginning. Your stories inspire us. Your courage fuels our fight for a just and equitable society. Together, we are writing a new chapter in our history – a history that honors every voice, every life."

The applause that followed was thunderous, reverberating through the very core of the nation.

As the year drew to a close, the Vanguard Coalition had not only dismantled a corrupt regime but had ignited a revolution of hope and unity across the United States. They were more than just superheroes; they were leaders of a new era – one defined by compassion, integrity, and a relentless pursuit of justice.

In the glow of a new dawn, the nation began to heal, and the Vanguard Coalition stood ready to guide them forward, reminding everyone that true power lay in the hands of the people. The legacy of Walker and his cronies would not be forgotten; it would serve as a catalyst for vigilance and advocacy – an enduring reminder that the fight for justice was a shared responsibility that every citizen must embrace.

25

Shadows of Fear

The winds of change swept through the halls of power not just in the United States but across the globe. The overthrow of President Walker and other top politicians, and the establishment of the Vanguard Coalition sent shockwaves that rippled through corrupt governments and corporations around the world, igniting a fear that had long simmered beneath the surface. As news reports celebrated the coalition's reforms, whispers of unease grew louder in the secretive chambers of power in nations where greed and oppression still thrived. The threat to their power imposed by the Vanguard couldn't be allowed to continue...

In a lavish office overlooking the skyline of London, Robert Sinclair, a high-ranking executive of a global pharmaceutical conglomerate, paced nervously. The fallout from the Vax-23 scandal had reached international proportions, and the company's stock had plummeted in the wake of revelations surrounding unethical practices. The unassailable titan of the industry now felt vulnerable, threatened by the rising tide of accountability sweeping through the United States.

"If the Vanguard can do this in the U.S.," Sinclair muttered, his voice low and tremulous, "what's stopping them from spreading their influence worldwide?" His fingers drummed anxiously on the mahogany desk, his mind racing with possibilities of unrest. He feared the awakening of other nations.

Across Europe, in a dimly lit meeting room in Moscow, a group of shadowy figures gathered around a large, oval table. The air was thick with cigar smoke and tension as Viktor Orlov, a notorious oligarch with fingers in many corrupt pies, presided over the meeting. His cold blue eyes scanned the room, glinting with malice.

"The Americans have awakened a sleeping giant," he said, his voice low and gravelly. "If they can expose corruption in their own government, they will ultimately turn their gaze upon us. We must act swiftly before they gain any more momentum." The room fell silent, the weight of his words sinking in like a stone in still water.

"Don't forget the whispers about Vax-23," one of Orlov's associates, a wiry man named Dmitri, chimed in. "If it is true that these individuals obtained abilities from it, others could too – powers that could rival those of the Vanguard. If more emerge, we will be out-matched."

Myla, a young analyst who had been quietly observing the powerful men around her, dared to speak. "What if we create our own response? If we can find those affected by Vax-23, we could harness their powers before they align with the Vanguard. We must infiltrate and turn this narrative in our favor." Her voice trembled slightly, a mix of fear and ambition igniting within her.

The oligarchs exchanged glances, contemplating her proposal. The idea of recruiting superhumans was as appealing as it was terrifying. Myla could see a flicker of interest in Orlov's steely gaze.

Meanwhile, in the dark underbelly of international espionage, other secret meetings took place between corrupt leaders, their paranoia simmering just below the surface. In a hushed conference room in Beijing, a senior government official tapped his fingers nervously on the table, the tension noticeable.

"The Vanguard may have inspired movements in our territories. We cannot let this happen," he warned, his voice barely above a whisper. "We need to deploy our resources to find out if there are other superhumans and bring them under our control before they align with the coalition."

Across the room, another official leaned in, his eyes gleaming with a mix of ambition and fear. "We should not only capture them; we should experiment. We have the technology to enhance their abilities, make them ours to command."

Back in the United States, the Vanguard Coalition remained focused on their mission, but they were not blind to the shadows lurking beyond their borders. Reports from intelligence agencies began to flood in, warning of potential threats from foreign powers reacting to the coalition's success.

Mark gathered the team in their headquarters, the once opulent space transformed into a vibrant community hub. The walls adorned with colorful murals celebrating unity and resilience stood in stark contrast to the dark realities they faced.

"We've received credible intel that several governments are beginning to view us as a threat," Mark announced, his voice steady but urgent. "They see our success as a rallying cry for their own people. This could spark global unrest."

Lydia, her brow furrowed in concentration, added, "They're frightened of losing control. If we can empower the disenfranchised in their countries, we might ignite revolutions similar to our own. That fear can also lead to desperate measures on their part."

Elara, her gaze distant, spoke up, "What if they find more people like us – with superhuman abilities... they could unleash those who have been impacted by Vax-23. Ones who haven't been able to control their powers... They could pose a threat to innocent lives and be used as pawns in their games."

Alex clenched his fists, the weight of responsibility heavy on his shoulders. "We need to be ready. If these regimes are truly afraid, they might try to retaliate in ways we can't predict. We must prepare for anything."

Mark stood before his team, his voice a steady anchor in the storm. "We cannot ignore the threat that lies ahead. If they strike, we need to be united. Our success cannot become a weapon against us. We must remain vigilant."

As the meeting adjourned, the air was thick with uncertainty. The Vanguard Coalition was a beacon of hope, but they were also a target. With corrupt governments tightening their grips and whispers of superhumans emerging across the globe, the stage was set for an impending confrontation that could change the world forever.

In preparation for the possibility of conflict, the coalition increased its outreach efforts, contacting international human rights organizations and supporting grassroots movements. They encouraged those affected by Vax-23 to come forward, providing a haven and assistance in harnessing their powers.

As the Vanguard Coalition strategized, ominous reports from global intelligence continued. The atmosphere grew increasingly tense, with rumors of uprisings, rogue experiments, and superhumans awakening worldwide.

"They think they are safe," a figure said, their voice low and dripping with malice. "Soon, the Vanguard will face a force they never expected. We will reclaim control." A chilling realization settled over the world: the fear of the Vanguard Coalition was only just beginning. The fight for justice would soon spiral into a battle against an unseen enemy; one born from the same shadows that had long oppressed the innocent. The stage was set, and the clock was ticking.

Acknowledgments

Becoming an author and publisher has always been a dream of mine. As a child, I would create stories and adorn them with "Monk Publishing," a name my Papa inspired based upon his nickname for me, "Monkey."

Thank you to my educators, family, and friends who have encouraged me over the years to write and publish.

Thank you, Nanny, a major support throughout my education and the development of my written skills, including editing countless college essays and reading to me so much as a child. Aunt Pearl, thank you for your creative inspiration and advice. Pearl and Nanny, your love for education and books is inspiring to many.

To my readers, thank you for supporting a new author.

A.B. Arch is the pen name of an author based out of the United States. With a background in criminal justice and psychology, she draws from her curiosity involving human interaction and emotion to write fiction and fantasy. After earning a doctorate in Clinical Psychology, she decided it was time to launch her lifelong dream of a publishing career. When she is not writing or working on other projects, she enjoys snowboarding, reading, traveling, experiencing new cultures and foods, and creating wonderful memories with her husband, friends, and family. Historical non-fiction is her favorite genre.

"The Awakening" is her first published book as an author. Inspired by her husband's delectation in fantasy and superheroes, and the global turmoil over the past few years, she felt inspired to write something that expressed the frustrations of everyday people, but in a fantasy/alternative history format. This book is the first in a series that aims to dig deeper into what lurks in the shadows of real life...

Do not fear to ask questions
or share inspiring stories.
– A.B. Arch